USA TODAY BESTSELLING AUTHOR

DALE MAYER

X-Ray in the Xanth

Lovely Lethal Gardens

REWIND 03

X-RAY IN THE XANTH: LOVELY LETHAL GARDENS REWIND, BOOK 3
Beverly Dale Mayer
Valley Publishing Ltd.

This is a work of fiction. Names, characters, places, brands, media, and incidents either are the product of the author's imagination or are used fictitiously. Any resemblance to actual events, locales, or persons, living or dead, is entirely coincidental.

ISBN-13: 978-1-778866-73-9
Print Edition

Books in This Series:

Zonked in the Zucchinis, Book 1
Yipped in the Yams, Book 2
X-Ray in the Xanth, Book 3
Weapon in the Watermelon, Book 4

Chapter 1

DOREEN SLEPT IN the next morning, only to wake up to find Mack standing in her bedroom doorway, grinning at her. She blinked several times and groaned. "What time is it?"

"It's eight."

"In the morning?" she asked, sitting up.

"Yes. I've been up most of the night. I slept for a few hours, but now I'm heading over to the office. I just thought I would pop in to check on you and to have a cup of coffee."

Still yawning, she grabbed her robe and headed down to the kitchen behind him.

He quickly set up the coffeepot and looked over at her. "For somebody who churns up all the chaos you cause," he muttered, "you should look a whole lot more exhausted, but instead you look absolutely beautiful." He leaned over, gave her a searing kiss, and muttered, "Come on. Move up the wedding date already, will ya?" She blinked several times as he placed a cup of coffee in front of her. Just then his phone rang, and he listened for a minute, quickly responded, then disconnected and groaned. "See? Now look what you've done."

"What have I done?" she asked.

"Everybody is bringing up all their own questions from other matters all over town and beyond, now that you've solved this case. They're looking for help for everything. Remember that envelope from under Lilybeth's bed?"

"You mean, the letter inside?"

"Yeah, and some pictures too?"

"Right, but I didn't get much chance to look at them before the chaos happened."

"Yeah, well, we blew them up, the photos, and one of the men knew where the garden was from one of those pictures, and they headed over there to see if they were right. They were supposed to finish up and to go home but couldn't leave it alone. They argued about the garden."

"What? Where was it?"

"I don't know, and I really don't have a clue why I should even tell you," Mack added in exasperation. "Nor do I have a clue what inspired them to grab a shovel and to dig around. But they did …"

"You better tell me. I found the photos, after all."

"You may have found them," Mack noted, "but Darren thought he knew where the pictures were taken from."

"And then they went and dug in that area?"

"Yeah, they did, mostly because Arnold was bugging him about it, saying he was wrong and didn't know. So, true to form, they made some ridiculous bet out of it, but anyway it didn't take Darren very long, and they dug up something."

"What was buried there?"

"Old X-rays."

"X-rays?"

"Yeah, but the old hard kind that they used way back when."

"Okay, if you say so. What difference does that make?"

"I don't know." Mack raised both hands. Then his phone buzzed, and he read the text message and groaned. "Well, now I do," he said, with a sigh.

"What is it?"

"Apparently they found a bone with the X-rays."

She started to grin.

"No," he ordered in exasperation, but she just cackled. "Our hands are full right now," Mack declared.

"That's good. Maybe by the time you're caught up, I'll have the X-ray mystery solved. By the way, what was planted in that garden?"

"I don't know. Do you want me to find out?"

"Yep, I do, indeed."

Several texts later, Mack groaned. "I don't know what these are." He pointed at them, as he held up his phone to show Doreen the image of a flower.

She looked at them and nodded. "They seem to be part of the chrysanthemum family."

"Maybe." He shrugged. "See? It doesn't work. You can't do an alliteration for this one. Besides, it won't be your case. It'll be mine."

"Really?" she asked, checking out the photos. "Looks to be an old bone."

He frowned as he pulled the picture back, realizing that the bone was there.

"It's part of a jawbone," she noted. He raised an eyebrow at her, and she nodded. "Elizabeth will love this one."

"No, she won't. Besides, you can't make an alliteration out of it. So you don't get to have anything to do with it."

She looked at him and smiled. "*X-ray in the Xanth*."

"What's a *xanth*?" he asked in confusion.

"Mums."

"Mums?"

"Yeah, chrysanthemums," she explained, with a beaming smile. "So, that's next."

"I don't care if it's next or not. That bone has been there for a very long time, so it and the X-rays can lay there for a little longer. I have to go finish up the mess from last night."

"Okay." She gave him a hug. "Now at least I know what's next on my list."

"Doesn't have to be," he protested. "You need to rest. You told me that you needed a rest before getting married."

"I do," she agreed, but then she grinned. "I just don't need a super big rest."

"Right," he muttered, with an eye roll, "as if I'll believe that."

"You should because now"—she rubbed her hands together—"we have *X-ray in the Xanth.*"

He leaned over, kissed her hard, and announced, "I'm going to work, and maybe that's just self-defense on my part."

"Call it what you want, but I've got my next cold case to work on."

"You do that. Just remember to get some rest, as you've got a wedding to plan." And, when the smile fell off her face, he laughed and laughed. "No pressure."

She smiled and nodded. "I really do appreciate you."

He gazed at her and nodded. "And I really appreciate you."

Chapter 2

A S SOON AS Mack walked out the door and headed to his truck, Doreen called him back and asked, "Where are Arnold and Darren working?" When he glared at her, she shrugged. "You and I both know that I'll find out, so you might as well help me sort out where they are. If nothing else, I can ask Richie where his grandson is working today."

He snorted at that. "*Right.* They're down at Higgles Park in Rutland."

Doreen grimaced. She knew the Rutland neighborhood within Kelowna. But that park? "Higgles Park? I don't know that one."

"I don't think it's called that anymore. It's a name the old-timers know, and it's supposed to be going through a rebeautification process."

"Ah, so Darren and Arnold digging there also helps out the city. So where is this park?"

He shrugged, smiling at the glare he got in return from Doreen. "Have a nice day," he exclaimed. And, with that, he walked to his truck, whistling a happy tune.

She frowned back at him. "Now you're just being mean."

He lifted a hand and waved, then got in his truck and drove away, a big grin still on his face.

She groaned as she stared at Mugs, as he slumped down at her feet. It seemed he also couldn't believe Mack had just done that.

Richard looked over from his front yard and called out to her in exasperation, "Now what? You guys are acting as if you've been married for eighty years already."

She gasped at him. "That's not fair," she cried out. "He's got a new case and won't tell me a thing about it."

Richard just stared at her, then shook his head and walked inside, slamming his front door behind him.

She frowned at Mugs, shaking her head. "How come nobody understands?" she muttered. She headed back inside to look up the location of Higgles Park. She'd never even heard of such a place. When she couldn't find anything about it online, she grew frustrated. How was that a thing? She contacted Nan, thinking, of all people, her grandmother ought to know something. "Hey, have you ever heard of a place in Rutland called Higgles Park?"

"Nope. Wait. … Maybe, but it's not called that anymore."

"I know," she muttered. "Mack wouldn't tell me what its name is now."

Nan went silent, then asked, "Is there a particular reason you're asking?"

"Of course I have a reason," Doreen declared in exasperation. "And I'm part of the reason they're down there, but Mack won't let me go be a part of it now."

"Of course not." Nan laughed at her. "He's trying to keep you away from his current case."

"I know that, which is also why I'm determined to find

out what I can, however I can. On that last case, a bunch of photos were found under Lilybeth's bed." She shook her head and continued. "In one of the photos, the location was recognized, and apparently Arnold and Darren headed down there to prove if it was or wasn't that location. While there, they found something worth getting out their shovels for, but all they will tell me is that they found a partial jawbone and some ancient X-rays."

"What?" Nan asked in astonishment.

"Exactly. So, in terms of things getting clearer, it's just getting murkier. I thought, if I could at least go down there, maybe I could talk to them."

Nan laughed. "Sounds good to me. I bet Richie knows where Darren is today. I'll check with him and get back to you right away. Meanwhile, I'll ask around to see if anybody remembers that Higgles Park location or knows its new name. As this area grew, where maybe five separate communities merged together, the lines shifted. So things became a little bit harder to sort out."

"I understand how that could happen," Doreen muttered, "but surely somebody knows something."

"Oh, we'll find somebody who knows something," Nan vowed, "but that doesn't mean anybody will be prepared to tell you about it. You know how Mack orders Darren to keep his mouth shut, especially when it comes to Richie's meddling."

"*Great*," she muttered.

As soon as they ended the call, Doreen could almost imagine her grandmother racing down the hallway, telling everybody that they had a new case—especially the Sherlock-hat-wearing crowd. That made it sound as if Nan were the town crier, spreading the good news that they could look forward to having something new and interesting to hear about. It's not that they were all bored out of their minds, but these mysteries were fun for them.

It was exciting to solve problems, particularly problems that had been set aside years ago. It's not that anything was unsolvable, but more a matter of new technology becoming available, along with people finally willing to talk. And, if people were willing to talk, Doreen was willing to listen, in whatever capacity that would be. Of course, that caused all kinds of other issues too.

Still, when Nan called back a little bit later, she shared, "It's up off the Belgo Road area. It used to be more of a baseball park with local games for the school kids than a real park."

Once Doreen got a rough idea of where it was, she thanked Nan and noted, "I'll take a drive up that way and see if I can come up with anything."

"Or we could come with you," Nan suggested eagerly.

"Who is *we*?" Doreen asked warily. "Whenever we get into these *we* things, it becomes a lot more complex."

Nan laughed. "Maybe just me then. I can fit in the car, even with all the animals."

"That you could. All right, I'll come down and pick you up in a few minutes." With that, she ended the call and started grabbing leashes for everybody. The animals were more than ready to head out on an adventure.

"You guys seem to think you've been deprived of excitement for the last day or two. While it's been so cold outside, we don't go outside as often each day. However, it hasn't been very long at all, you know?"

Yet she had to admit that she was just as eager and anxious to get moving as they were, even though the cold weather sucked her breath away as she stepped outside each time. She bundled up again, yet it still probably wasn't enough. As soon as she had everybody loaded up in her car, she drove to Rosemoor, found Nan already standing outside, pacing impatiently on the sidewalk. At least she was dressed for the winter temps here in BC.

The second Doreen stopped her car, Nan dashed inside. When Doreen frowned at her, Nan pointed. "You need to drive this thing out of here, before everybody finds out that we've gone without them."

Doreen rolled her eyes but quickly backed out of the parking lot and took off.

Almost immediately Nan's phone rang. She turned to Doreen and nodded. "See? Now they will all be asking where I am."

"Surely you can come up with something. However, since you were seeking information on the park, somebody probably spilled the beans, and now here you are, absconding without them."

"Exactly," Nan exclaimed, with glee.

Such satisfaction filled her tone that Doreen had to laugh. "You are too funny." She shook her head.

"You've got to have some excitement in your life at this stage," Nan explained, then settled in and looked around to see all the animals.

Thaddeus poked his head out of Doreen's hair. "Thaddeus loves Nan. Thaddeus loves Nan."

"Ah, thank you, sweetheart," Nan replied, stroking his soft feathers. "It's always so lovely to see you."

The two of them kept up a nonsensical conversation, while Doreen tried to navigate her way to the Belgo Road area. "Why is Belgo Road cut into so many pieces?" she asked in frustration, as she took yet another wrong turn.

"When growth happens, city planners happen," Nan stated.

"This is not a *planned* city area," she replied in frustration. "Why are there so many intersections where it's one street name on one side and a completely different name on the other? Surely nobody could think that was *planning*."

"It was planned," Nan stated, with a nod, "but not necessarily *well* planned."

Doreen groaned. "The whole city is a mess that way."

"Yet it's much better when you're up here."

"Maybe," Doreen muttered, "but, if you looked up Belgo on the map, it's all over the place."

Nan nodded. "And you're right there. It's definitely a bit of a hodgepodge, but we'll get there."

It didn't take too many more wrong turns, until suddenly Doreen hit the brakes and pulled to the side of the road. When Nan eyed her curiously, Doreen pointed up ahead to the police vehicle blocking the road.

Nan chuckled. "See? Sometimes we don't even need maps. We just have to spot any black-and-white cruisers."

"That's terrible," she muttered, "but still, it's a good indication that we could be in the right place."

"Could be," Nan agreed. "Looks very much like we must be at the scene of the crime."

"We've been wrong before," Doreen noted, as she hopped out, then walked over to where the policemen were standing, as crime scene tape was being rolled off in the park.

Arnold looked up and grinned. "We took bets on how long it would take you."

Immediately Nan stepped up. "What? You took bets without me?"

Arnold frowned at her and grumbled, "Yeah, we figured at least that way we had a chance to win."

She snorted at that and nodded. "Good thinking, you know? Good thinking."

Arnold practically preened, as if he were happy with the compliment.

Doreen sighed. "Are you guys done chitchatting?"

"Oh, we're done all right," Arnold declared, "but it's all good. We're having a grand old time here."

"I heard about the jawbone."

"Of course, which is why you're here." Darren groaned. "We're not allowed to give you any information."

"But it's a cold case," Doreen clarified, rubbing her hands together.

"What makes you think it's a cold case?" Arnold asked, glaring at her.

"Because the body's been lying here, and it's cold, well at least a body part is here."

Darren snorted at that response, and Arnold looked a little confused. Darren shook his head. "That might work for Mack, but it sure ain't gonna work for us."

"No, maybe not, but I can phone the captain and get access to this, if I want."

They frowned at each other, then at her, but nodded. "That you can probably do," Darren noted.

"And it wouldn't be a bad idea if you did because it would cover our butts," Arnold added, giving her a stare.

"Do you think it's really a problem? Me being here?" she asked, astonished. "I mean, all I'm doing is … observing."

"Yeah, for how long?" Arnold asked, shaking his head. "From what we know about you, your *observing* has a way of ending up becoming something else very quickly."

"Oh, you mean, like solving the crime?" she asked, tongue-in-cheek.

He rolled his eyes. "We don't have time to do any of that other stuff," he muttered, shaking his head.

Doreen thought she detected a note of envy in his tone. "And that's one of the reasons why I do it," she replied. "Because you guys don't have the time or the extra manpower, but these victims still need to have a voice."

"Maybe," he muttered, looking over at Darren.

Darren shrugged. "As far as I'm concerned, I don't see anything wrong with Doreen looking around, and she would eventually find out from Mack anyway."

"And, if not Mack," she added, "definitely the captain." She pulled out her phone, sent the captain a text regarding the Higgles Park body part. Then she looked over at the two men. "We do know it's human, correct?"

"Yes," Darren confirmed. "Obviously we haven't had an anthropologist come in, and I don't think we'll need to in terms of identifying whether it's a human body part or not because it was clearly a human jawbone."

"Right." Doreen nodded. "Any other bone and you may have had a question from a layman, but the human jawbone pretty well makes it clear."

"It really does," he agreed, shrugging. "Nothing is quite so easily identifiable."

"Except a human hand or foot," she pointed out, looking at him.

He sighed and nodded. "Anyway, we found a jawbone, so a jawbone is a jawbone is a jawbone."

She smiled. They were right in that a jawbone was definitely fairly clear-cut. As she watched, Darren and Arnold resumed with the digging. "Are you guys doing all the digging? Don't we have anybody in forensics to dig this up?"

"Yeah, the coroner was here already, and she's coming back with a crew to help, but it's not as if she'll grab a shovel and give us a hand."

"I would grab a shovel and give you a hand," Doreen offered, "but I would have to hold Nan back if I did."

At that, the others looked over at Nan and shook their heads. Darren pointed out, "See what we mean? Doreen's here for the glory, … not the work."

"Hey, I would help dig, but I also know that you guys wouldn't let me dig," she replied. "If Mack found out that you gave me a shovel, you know how much trouble you'll all be in."

"Yeah, we sure do," Darren muttered, "so you don't get to help." Just then he stepped back and gridded off another section. "We're not necessarily doing the final grid work. That'll be on the coroner, except …"

"Except what?" asked a woman behind Doreen.

She turned to see Elizabeth walking toward her.

A hard smile cut into her face as Elizabeth muttered, "Of course you're here."

Chapter 3

DOREEN NODDED. "CONSIDERING I'm the one who found the picture that revealed this crime scene, yeah, I am here."

Elizabeth frowned at her. "Now that's fascinating."

"That's what I thought," Doreen agreed, with a nod. "I mean, there's just a little bit of something every time I turn around."

"The fact that you found the photograph, and now we found this jawbone is huge," Elizabeth replied. "It's also sad."

"We don't know a whole lot about it, do we?" Doreen asked.

"No, what I can tell you is that the X-ray is *old*, old."

Doreen interrupted, "Was it just one? I was confused about the number of X-rays found."

Elizabeth shook her head. "Nope. Just one came to my lab."

Doreen frowned. "So just a miscommunication?"

Elizabeth shrugged. "It happens more than you can imagine. It's been preserved and even seems to be laminated. However, the lamination started to peel off, so somebody put it in what appears to be a liquid plastic coating. So I don't know if we'll be able to date the actual X-ray after so much deterioration."

"So, somebody was trying to preserve the X-ray?" Doreen asked. "That seems a bit much. What was on that X-ray worth preserving?"

"That's the fascinating thing," Elizabeth began, warming up to the subject. Then she frowned and asked in a low tone, "Will I get in trouble by talking to you?"

"That's the never-ending question when dealing with Doreen," Arnold chimed in. "We would like to say no, but …"

"But you don't know that." Darren completed the sentence and started to walk away.

"No, I don't know that," Arnold stated, "but, since it's Doreen, she can get away with a lot more than anybody else."

Doreen frowned. Arnold was definitely having trouble with her getting her way all the time. "It's also a cold case," Doreen pointed out. "Which you well know is what I am working on, and the last one was certainly with the captain's permission."

"Sure, but that was the last one," Darren pointed out, coming back to join them, having heard what she had said. "We very much would like to know if you're approved to be working on this one."

As it was, Elizabeth had already pulled out her phone and was making a call. She turned back, looked at Doreen and the others, and announced, "The captain's fine with it."

Doreen beamed. "No reason for him not to be," she stated, as she once more rubbed her hands together. She looked over at Nan, who was looking absolutely thrilled to be hooked into another case and as involved as she already was.

"Now," Doreen asked the coroner, "male or female?"

"Male," Elizabeth replied. She looked back at her. "You and I will have a talk one day. You really should have gone into my field."

"Maybe," Doreen conceded, "but my life took a very different pathway."

At that, the two men snorted, and Arnold added, "Yeah, she just became one of those nosy types, who suddenly gets all kinds of success."

"Suddenly?" she asked in a wry tone.

"*Suddenly* is relative, I guess," Darren noted, shaking his head. "I know you deserve all the credit you get. It's just so amazing to us that we're even having this conversation because we're not even working on cold cases."

"It is a fascinating field, and I would absolutely love to be working on more of them," Elizabeth shared.

Arnold smiled. "But you're not because you're still at the beginning of your career and working in a place that lacks the depth for specialties like that. Maybe when you've got a few more years in, you'll get there."

"Unless you go somewhere that has a Doreen on the loose," Darren added.

Elizabeth burst out laughing. "There are worse things in life than to work for a department that doesn't have any missing person cases, unidentified bodies, or cold cases that were never solved," she declared. "There's always Penticton, Vernon, the Kamloops, and Merritt. If you get to be good at it, you can go anywhere."

"Maybe that's what you should do," Darren suggested, turning to look at Doreen.

She shrugged. "I'm not going anywhere. This is home for me, and I'm staying here."

"Particularly because Mack is here."

She blushed and Nan chuckled. "Even if she won't admit it," Nan muttered.

"Hey, I'm marrying the man, so that should be enough admitting."

Elizabeth smiled at her and asked, "Are you engaged to be married?" She sounded thrilled.

Doreen nodded. "Yes, and it's a fairly recent event," she noted, twisting the ring on her finger. "I'm still getting used to it."

"Nothing to really get used to, is there?" Elizabeth asked.

"There is because I was in a pretty-ugly divorce, a quite recent one that ended up in a huge mess," she explained. "In the midst of all that, my husband was murdered, and these guys thought I'd killed him, of course," she added, turning to glare at them.

Both the men shook their heads. "Nope, we never thought that, but we still had to do our due diligence."

Doreen's shoulders slumped, and she nodded. "So, they did their due diligence, and I ended up helping them solve my soon-to-be ex-husband's murder," she shared with Elizabeth. "Anyway I warned Mack that I won't be pushed into an early wedding, though the people around me," she shared, shooting a glare at Nan, "don't seem to be listening."

"Nope, we sure aren't," Nan declared.

"Neither is Mack." Arnold cackled. "He wants you locked down and tied up, so you can't run away."

"I won't say that he doesn't feel that way, but he knows that I love him," Doreen stated. "So, no matter what everyone makes of it, … it's really not an issue. And Mack has been extremely patient so far."

"Yeah, you're not kidding," Arnold muttered. "Look at all that you've got him into."

"You mean, at all that I've gotten myself into," she amended.

"Yeah, that too." He chuckled.

"That is all very fascinating," Elizabeth said, "but it won't solve our current issue."

"No, and I am very fascinated with that right now," Doreen replied, as she looked around. "There are more than a few aspects to this case that I'm curious about."

"Such as?" Elizabeth asked.

"Is there only one body part? Or do you think parts from an entire body are spread out here too? What is the age of the decedent at death, and how long has the jawbone been buried here? It would also help to have a cause of death," she noted, "and—"

Arnold nodded. "ID of the body would help too, if we're asking for miracles," he interjected, adding to the list of questions. And then he saw Doreen's expression, suggesting he had missed something. When he glared at her, she rolled her eyes at him.

"Significance of the X-ray. You seem to be forgetting that."

Elizabeth looked up and beamed. "See? You're perfect for this."

"I am fascinated by that X-ray. The fact that it was preserved or meant to be preserved suggests that somebody needed proof, … either of injuries caused, injuries received, or"—she hesitated—"I hate to say it, *blackmail.*"

"Ooh, I like the way you think," Elizabeth said, laughing.

Immediately Arnold pulled his pants up over his ample girth and acknowledged, "She's right. Those are pretty important pieces."

Elizabeth nodded. "So, how are you guys doing on this grid work?"

"I think we've pretty well done what you asked for," Arnold responded, pointing out beyond the established grids. "So, anything beyond this, you told us not to get any closer."

"Right, I don't want you any closer than this just because of the proximity to where the bones could be. So, estimating a six-foot-tall plus man, presumably buried intact, yet with some bones disturbed by wildlife, we would figure it'll be somewhere in here." And, with that, she got down to work with much smaller tools, her team right beside her. They looked at Doreen a couple times, but she just smiled and didn't say anything. For once, Nan decided she would stay mostly quiet too.

Doreen had to admit she appreciated Nan's reticence because this was not the time to be causing trouble. As it was, Elizabeth's guess had worked out quite well, since before long she had found the feet of the man. The bones barely held together. Doreen asked if she could step closer.

Elizabeth nodded. "Just don't touch anything."

"No, I won't," she said, as she bent down beside the female coroner. "Fascinating."

"What's fascinating?" Elizabeth asked.

"As a layperson not in this field," Doreen shared, "I find it fascinating that the bones are somehow held together."

"Most of that is due to the way we dug around it," Elizabeth explained, "and we'll have to pull out these bones one by one." She looked back at the forensics crew. "Are you guys ready to do that? Need a body bag over here or an evidence box, but I need something to put all this into."

It ended up being a carton, and Elizabeth very carefully lifted out each bone and securely placed it inside for safekeeping and transport.

As Doreen sat back and watched her, she whispered, "It's nice to see the amount of care you give the bones, even after all these years."

"In many cases," Elizabeth explained, "it's extra care just because of the many years involved. When you think about it, this poor man has been here for a very long time, completely unknown and uncared about."

"Oh, he's been cared about," Doreen countered, "but for all the wrong reasons."

Elizabeth stared at her.

Doreen nodded. "The killer cared about him, even if just as a question that kept popping up in the back of his mind—wondering if it'll ever be found, wondering if he'll ever get caught," she suggested. "Of course I'm working on the premise that he's still alive and that he will pay for this."

"Do we know for sure that this man was murdered?" Nan asked in a reasonable tone.

Moments earlier, Elizabeth had opened up the area to the spine. She took a look, then turned back to them. "The ribs appear to be crushed, and the spine is broken. So there's your answer to that." Elizabeth turned to Nan.

Nan winced. "I presume that was fatal."

"Pretty close," Elizabeth replied, with a nod. "Don't know his age yet, but there could be extenuating circumstances. I also have to see whether these injuries were pre- or postmortem."

"Right, that would change things entirely," Doreen muttered. Then she sighed. "Even if postmortem, it won't get anybody off the hook."

"No, it won't," Elizabeth agreed, looking at Doreen. "So, I'm glad you're on the case. This person needs justice."

"And how long has he been here?" Doreen muttered, almost to herself.

Elizabeth shook her head. "I'll have to get back to you on that."

Doreen continued to stare at the broken spine.

Elizabeth asked, "What are you thinking?"

Doreen grimaced and tilted her head. "From the looks of it, and I could be wrong, this appears to be a very tall individual, like six and a half feet at a guess."

"I can confirm that, once we measure the femur," the coroner shared, pointing out the bone. "But, yes, that's close enough for now. What difference does that make?"

"I'm just considering the weight, the dead weight, I mean. If this man was as badly broken as this, how does someone carry him here and then bury him? And why here? Why no animal damage, at least nothing obvious yet?" Turning to look around, she added, "It's not a very deep grave."

"It's a good four feet," Elizabeth noted. Then she turned to face the two policemen. "Wasn't some work being done in this area?"

"Yes," Arnold stated. "a fair bit of work was being done here, with all the topsoil graded off. I suspect that a memorial park will be placed here."

"Not necessarily," Doreen replied, "because this looks to be cleared for a massive development." She looked around the site. "This body was probably buried a good six feet under at the time of digging this grave."

The coroner nodded, looking around too. "That could

be, but ..."

"I know," Doreen muttered, "that's not the issue. The real issue is who this man is and whether we can get any DNA off him. Will he match any of our missing people or cold cases, and who or what caused his death? These bodily injuries look like the result of a car crash," she guessed, "or something heavy falling on him, or him falling and landing on something equally heavy."

The coroner smiled at her. "And I would agree with any of those in theory," she noted, "but I still need to take the bones back to my table and analyze them."

Doreen hesitated before asking, "And is this something that you do? ... Or is this something that a specialist is brought in for?"

"I can do it," Elizabeth stated. "If I find that I'm past my own skill level, then we'll bring somebody in."

"I'm not trying to step on toes or anything," Doreen added.

"Nope, but a specialist is a specialist. In some things, I'm not a specialist," Elizabeth stated, with a smile.

"And apparently, neither am I," Doreen admitted, with a chuckle.

"Yes, you are," Nan argued. "You've done wonders on all these cold cases."

"You've also done wonders getting into trouble," Arnold pointed out, with an eye roll. "You might want to keep that in mind."

"So, what are you saying, Arnold? That I'm a specialist in finding trouble?" Doreen cried out.

"Sure. And I think Mack would agree with that assessment."

She glared at him, but, from behind her, Mack declared,

"And that's exactly what my assessment would be."

She turned, looked at him, and beamed. "There you are."

"Yeah, it's funny," he pointed out, with a knowing look in her direction, "how some of us do have to attend to other issues." He looked over at Arnold and Darren. "If you're done here, the captain wants you back. We've got a triple-car pileup on Highway 97."

The two men's eyes widened, and they hurried off, taking their shovels with them. Mack snagged one of the shovels as they went by, then turned to Elizabeth and smiled. "Hey, Elizabeth."

"Hey, Mack," she replied, with a beaming smile. "Aren't you a sight for sore eyes? I just heard you're engaged to our resident sleuth here."

He smiled, walked over to Doreen, and, putting an arm around her waist, he tucked her up in a hug. "That I am, and, even with my best of intentions, I keep trying to get her to stay out of trouble, but—"

"It doesn't happen," Elizabeth finished his sentence for him and nodded. "I get it. She's got an incredibly good eye for this work though."

"I know," he agreed, "which is also why the captain keeps letting her in on the cases." He turned and glared at her.

She smiled. "Love you too, sweetie."

He chuckled. "We'll talk about that when you give me a date."

"I already told you, fourth quarter."

Nan looked at her and asked, "Fourth quarter of what?"

"Fourth quarter of this year, but, if people keep bugging me, maybe it'll be next year. Take it or leave it."

Elizabeth howled. "She'll keep you on your toes."

"She already does," Mack said, with a groan. "Now, what have you got for me?" he asked, turning to the coroner.

Elizabeth smirked. "Why don't you ask your girlfriend?"

He stared at her for a moment, then turned to Doreen. "Technically fiancée, … but seriously?"

Doreen shrugged. "I'm just getting a few bits and pieces of info for myself," she muttered. "I'm not stepping on toes."

"You're stepping on as many toes as you think you can step on," Mack declared.

"Okay, okay, okay," she muttered. "We've got a male." She looked down at the bones. "And my guess, not hers, just me talking. I'll say middle-aged, somewhere between midthirties and midfifties."

Elizabeth raised one eyebrow. "We've got a crush-type injury, but it definitely reeks of foul play just because of the burial," she noted with a shrug, "and I really want to know what that X-ray has to do with anything."

"Maybe the X-ray of his injuries," Mack suggested to Elizabeth.

"I haven't had a chance to look at it," she noted, "but it is possible. Although why someone would have them with him out here is another thing."

"What I don't know," Doreen added, "is how long this poor man has been here. And, of course, he didn't get here on his own."

"No, but from what's left around here," Elizabeth pointed out, "you won't get a whole lot of information."

"Right," Doreen muttered. "I keep hoping that we'll end up with some clear-cut case, but that never happens."

Elizabeth laughed. "For this one, definitely not. But you were accurate to a certain extent on the general age of the decedent. I just can't confirm anything yet," she shared, turning to look at Doreen, "until I get the bones back on my table."

"Right." Doreen nodded.

Elizabeth hesitated before speaking. "Every once in a while, I do let people into my autopsy room."

Doreen was thrilled, grinning, a gleam in her eye.

Beside her, Mack groaned. "Are you sure you want to do that, Doreen?"

Doreen shrugged. "Hey, it'll be fun. It's not as if anything is gruesome or upsetting on this one."

Elizabeth nodded. "We'll just be looking at bones, after all."

"Yeah, we're just looking at bones," Doreen repeated, as she stared down at the dismally small number of them. "Hard to think of a life being completely stripped down to just this."

"It is, isn't it?" Elizabeth agreed. "But we'll find out what happened to him, and then his family can rest easy." She smiled at Doreen. "At least, I presume that's your goal."

"Absolutely, that's always my goal."

"It's *our* goal," Mack stated, with a sigh. "Let's not forget that the police are on the case too."

"Nobody's forgotten anything," Nan piped up. "I think all they want is to know that Doreen is on it as well, you know, to confirm it gets solved."

Mack's shoulders slumped, and he let out an audible groan as he looked over at Doreen, who walked up, slipped her fingers into his, and whispered, "I'm happy to work with you."

His lips twitched. "Now, if that meant you were sitting at a desk, doing online research, I would be happy with that too. However, you have this penchant for going off on these tangents of yours, then chaos breaks loose—very, very quickly."

Chapter 4

DOREEN DROPPED OFF Nan and came home, and with the captain's permission, spent all afternoon poring through the online database of missing persons among the cold cases, looking to see if she could connect any to this poor man reduced to a few bones and one very old X-ray. Of course not all the cold cases had been digitized. When she couldn't find anything, she was more than a little stumped. She figured she could get the captain to authorize her to go through the paper files. Yet she groaned at the thought. After all, she had heard rumors about them no longer being in any particular order—alphabetical, chronological, even segregated by crimes. Doreen shook her head at the thought of going through those physical records manually.

When Mack called her a little later, she asked, "Did you get any ID on the man?"

"Nope, not yet."

She groaned. "How can anybody not miss someone like that?"

"Because he could have come from anywhere across the country. He could have come up from the States, or he could have come down from Alaska, for all we know. Remember that, just because they end up here, it doesn't mean they started here."

"Right, I wasn't really thinking that he wouldn't be a local." She frowned. "I guess I should be thinking broader."

"Something like this, … that's been here this long, where nobody is tracking it, you have to think everywhere," he murmured.

"It is unnerving to see how quickly an entire body, especially somebody huge like that," she explained, "literally somebody your size, is reduced down to a few bones."

"It wasn't a short time frame though," he pointed out. "That body has been there a lot of years. We did check, and some excavation work was done in that area about twenty years ago, looking at developing out there."

"And yet it wasn't found then? How is that a thing?"

"It wasn't found because they didn't go deep enough."

"Right, of course not," she mumbled. "That's frustrating though."

"You can't let it get to you," he pointed out.

"I know," she grumbled, "but it needs to get to me a certain degree. Otherwise I won't maintain any sanity doing this stuff."

"That is one of the things I worry about with you," he shared. "We want to know that you're okay doing this. You aren't trained, and you don't have the experience to handle this constant barrage of the dark reality of humanity."

"I understand," she murmured, "and sometimes I do worry about that. Then something else happens, and I just love the puzzles and the chase. … After we find the killer, they pay for their crime. Then we also have closure for somebody else." She nodded. "And I realize how much it's all worth it."

"And it is worth it," he agreed. "I just need to know that you won't wind up distraught over it all. I can't have it on my conscience if it all gets to you, and you can't find any separation from it. That just can't happen on my watch, Doreen. It can't."

"Right, and I'm fine," she said, and she was. "I get that. I just took a break, had a cup of tea, trying to get some perspective. Plus, I can always call you to remind me that I get too close to these victims at times. Yet, sure, it's upsetting to think that this poor man has been here all this time, but, more than that, it's also important to remember that we are here now, and we can help him," she explained.

"That's a good way to look at it. However, I don't have any answers for you, or even any ideas at the moment. It'll take a bit of a time for Elizabeth to go over the bones, and, if she's not confident with her ability to handle them, … then we'll call in a specialist."

"She seems pretty capable though."

"Capable, yes, but we also need a solid determination on the time frame as to the man's death," he noted.

"Not really," she noted. "Even if we get a solid determination on time of death, we'll still be within what? A five-year range?"

"Possibly," he conceded. "If nothing indicates an exact time frame, then, yeah, that could be what we're looking at."

"There's the X-ray," she pointed out.

"What about it?"

"The X-ray should give us some idea of time."

"Maybe," he conceded.

"Plus, somebody made an attempt to preserve it," she pointed out, "so …"

"But the X-ray didn't have any identifying marks on

them back then."

"Oh. … I was hoping a company name and a date or something showed where and when the X-ray was taken, or at least by whom. Then we could track it down or have some idea if they could carbon-date it or something."

"Carbon-date it?" he repeated, with a chuckle. "So, you seem to be diving deep on this one."

"There's a certain manner of handling an X-ray, right? … I mean, you can't just recycle those," she pointed out. "They have silver or whatever other stuff on them, and they have to be treated differently. I would presume recycled by a company who specializes in that."

"That's interesting," Mack noted, "so that would be a place to start, to see if they can identify when this image may have been taken."

"Exactly," she said.

"I'm at the hospital in the X-ray department right now."

"But I don't imagine they would be recycling them," she pointed out. "They would ship them out to somebody else, I would think."

"Probably so." With that said, they soon ended the call.

Doreen spent the rest of the afternoon contemplating what it would take for somebody to kill someone and then to hide a body like that. It's not as if she wasn't used to the idea by now with other cold cases solved, but something about seeing that man discarded in such a huge grave and somebody knowing about it for all these years really bothered her.

She was often on the outskirts of these cases at this point. But now, by being more intimately involved from the start, seeing his remains, seeing the care Elizabeth took with them, made Doreen sad. Yet she wanted to do the best that she could for him.

It was just heartbreaking to think of this poor man lying there all these years, completely undetected, and yet somebody knew he was there. Somebody was not at all worried about him, only worried about themselves, worried their crime would ultimately be discovered. As the years passed, the murderer presumably got complacent over the whole thing, thinking they got off scot-free. She was really hoping that wouldn't be the case. She just didn't have any way to move forward yet, a fact that bothered her as well.

As she went through the online history of the park, it had been used as an old ball game field. A favorite place for the local teams to go play. Even before that it had been mostly owned by the Crown. At one point, it had been opened up for a public sale, either part of the green space for this new development back then, or who knows? Perhaps it would become something completely different.

It was really hard to tell from these old records. However, with the body having now been found, it would bring everything on any pending development project to a grinding halt. Yet she knew it wouldn't be for long. These things tended to be dealt with relatively quickly, at least she hoped so for their sake. There was nothing quite so irritating and frustrating as having to deal with all these delays. Even if the residents had a better idea of what was going on, there still needed to be some level of transparency.

She wanted to bug Elizabeth for answers but knew that wouldn't get Doreen very far and could potentially damage a burgeoning friendship and a great resource. Elizabeth would call her when she had anything to report. So, Doreen bided her time, even though it was hard to do.

When Nan called her later, Doreen muttered, "Sorry, I don't have an update."

"Of course not," Nan noted, but a wealth of disappointment filled her tone too.

"This stuff takes time, Nan." Doreen had to smile at herself because she was telling her grandmother exactly what she had been working at convincing herself of.

"I get that," Nan admitted, "but really there should be something."

"You already know what we found out at the scene."

"Which wasn't much," she pointed out.

"No, it sure wasn't," she agreed, "and that's a concern too, if this poor man was buried there all that time."

"I know. It's horrible," Nan cried out.

"And you don't know of anybody who went missing years ago? Not that we have a date range for the time of death yet."

"I love how you make it sound as if I was even aware of all this," Nan replied. "And, no, I have no idea."

"But somebody must have known him, even if he was visiting here, right? Especially if he had been living here but was leaving town and going back to another location."

"He was very tall, and that's one thing we have going for us. That sets him apart," Nan noted.

"There are still a lot of tall men here."

"Not back in our youth there weren't," Nan declared, with a snort. "I mean, generations are getting taller, but we don't know how old this man was or how long he was there. You guesstimated his age at roughly thirty-something to fifty-something. Even if we take him at his youngest, thirty-something, tack on maybe fifty years ago he was buried there, then he could still come in somewhere around Richie's age or so, I would suspect."

"Then we know who to talk to at least," Doreen replied.

"That would be a start."

"But he's still reeling from the last one," Nan stated worriedly.

"That's true. I was so hoping he would have some time to recover between cases."

Nan chuckled. "Of course you were."

"I would give him a little bit of time," Doreen muttered. "I mean, obviously he's had a rough go."

"It's not even that so much. I think it's just that life has caused so many people to struggle, and yet we don't quite realize what is happening in this town to other people. And that's hard to hear about, especially after the fact, when we could have possibly helped them earlier."

"Of course," Doreen agreed. "Like Mack was just telling me, he doesn't want me to get down and depressed by working all these cold cases. We don't want that for you and Richie and the others in your special club at Rosemoor either. However, we don't want anybody getting away with murder."

"Apparently somebody did," Nan muttered.

"I know, and the problem could be, at some point in some future cold case, we'll find out that the people responsible for someone's death are already dead and gone and don't have to pay the price. Speaking of not having to pay, did you hear that Bernie Winters is in the hospital?"

"That's karma for all the times his wife ended up there," Nan grumbled, with a sigh. "Yet she never reported him for beating her up all the time, and she never left him either. What a sorry excuse for a husband. Now she's long dead, and he will never be put in prison, which is definitely where he belongs," Nan muttered.

Doreen sighed. "It's sad, isn't it?"

"We've got to find this person who killed the body in the park now, before he gets away with everything too."

"I'm working on it," Doreen said. "With the captain's permission, I've been going through missing persons' files in BC, and, so far, I haven't come up with anybody who fits the description."

"And that initial physical description could be wrong. We're still in the estimating phase," Nan pointed out. "We wouldn't want to make a mistake on that."

"It's not even about making a mistake at this point," Doreen clarified, "because I don't have much in the way of parameters."

"I know, and that sucks."

Doreen felt it too because that seemed to be the general consensus for the rest of the day.

He chuckled. "If that's a yes, I'll be there in … maybe thirty. Or do you need longer?"

"No, thirty is fine." She stopped and asked, "Can the animals come?"

"I figured it was probably the easiest way to keep you out of trouble," he admitted. "And they do appear to do a rather decent job at that."

She snorted. "I'm sure they think I need a whole lot more looking after than I really do."

"Oh, but I agree with them," Mack added. "So I won't argue against that. I'll be there soon."

And, with that, he ended the call.

Chapter 6

DOREEN JUMPED OUT of bed, looked at the animals, and announced, "Time to eat, and we need to do it fast—or we'll have to convince Mack to stop and pick up something on the way."

She raced downstairs, fed them, and, with everybody busily munching away, she grabbed her coffee and managed to get one cup halfway down before he pulled into her driveway. She put on her extra layers to protect her from the cold weather. With the animals not protesting, now picking up on her excitement, she headed them all out to his vehicle.

He smiled at her, petting all the animals, and asked, "You ready to go?"

"More or less. I wasn't sure if we would stop and pick up coffee or what."

"We can," he said agreeably. "Absolutely no reason not to."

With a beaming smile, she nodded. "I did manage to get almost one cup of coffee but only that."

He gave her a fat smile. "Right. Let's go then."

Soon they hit the nearest drive-through, and very quickly she was nursing a large hot coffee and smiling, quite content to be where she was today.

"You look as if this is quite the field trip," he noted, glancing at her sideways.

She nodded. "And a good one," she admitted. "I'm really happy to be here today."

"Good to know. Normally you're not quite so agreeable."

"Ah." She nodded. "Not about going to the department to give a statement or to share my ideas that haven't worked out in my head yet, no. But today? I get to come out with you to the crime scene, so that's a whole different story."

"I hadn't considered that," he muttered. He smiled and asked, "Did you get any breakfast?"

She shook her head. "No, I fed the animals. Then the choice for me was coffee or food."

He pulled into another drive-through and ordered breakfast sandwiches for both of them.

She laughed. "So, was that something you were planning on doing already, or something you just figured out that we needed, since I hadn't eaten?"

"Not eating," he stated, staring her down, "will burn you through blood sugars and make you even more tired than you can imagine. We have to be prepared for anything, and that means you must have food in your stomach."

"I'm good with that," she replied, giving him a pleased smile.

When the breakfast sandwiches were handed to him, she suggested, "Can we just go to the park and eat there?"

"We can."

And that's what they ended up doing. With the animals outside with them, she walked them over to a tree stump nearby, where she sat and proceeded to polish off her breakfast sandwich. As she crumbled up her empty wrapper, she looked over at him and asked, "How come they're so … *moreish*? As in, I could eat more?"

He smiled. "It goes along with the whole setting, doesn't it? It's an outing. It's fun, and occasionally … it's nice to have a treat," he added, "but you are right. They are *more-ish*."

"Yet you only had one," she noted, frowning at him.

"Only needed one," he replied, with a shrug. "I'm a big guy, but that doesn't mean that I need to eat all the time, every time."

"Which means you had breakfast earlier."

"Which means I had breakfast earlier," he agreed, with a nod.

"I wasn't expecting this invitation today, so I was still in bed."

"Really?" he asked, frowning at her.

She nodded. "I had my laptop open, and the animals were around me, but we weren't pushing on anything in particular just yet."

"That's not a bad thing either," he said. "You can always relax, as you decide which *something* you can be working on."

"That's what I figured, but then you called. So I jumped up, fed them, and carried on."

He smiled and nodded. "The animals appear to be totally okay with spending some time out here with us."

"Are you kidding?" she asked, with a chuckle. "You're their favorite visitor. So, as far as they're concerned, any time you come, it just means fun times. Plus, I want them with me. They are all very special to me."

"Of course they are," he said. "In many ways, they're the

reason you survived every attack over the last eight or nine months."

"I definitely survived, and they are the reason I did."

Immediately his expression dropped. "No matter how much I try to keep you safe …"

"And I appreciate all your efforts. I do. Plus, I am doing my best to stay safe too," she admitted. "At least I'm trying to …" He gave her an eye roll at that. She chuckled. "So, what will we do here?"

"I want to get a bunch of photos of the lay of the land, so I can compare the area over the years," he explained. "Just backup information for any potential court case, you know, trying to get on top of it before we end up buried in so much other stuff."

"So while we're waiting for the information to come back from Elizabeth, we're doing some of the basic prep work for a trial."

"That's a good way to put it," he agreed. With the animals walking at their sides, he took a bunch of photos and measurements.

She had been quiet for a long while, but now she broke the silence. "It just seems so odd that somebody that size could disappear."

"Not really. What if he was driving down to the coast and never told anyone? What if he and his wife split, and he just decided he didn't want to live here anymore? I mean, there are all kinds of possibilities."

"But sad ones," she said.

He glanced at her and nodded. "Potentially sad ones. If we get into specifics, then a lot of life can be sad."

Her face fell. "I know. … I guess I'm still looking for happy endings."

Startled, he smiled at her. "That's a very interesting concept, considering you're the one who so often finds such very unhappy endings."

"Yet I think that finding closure for everybody is what makes me happy at some point," she clarified. "Obviously we don't want these murders to continue."

"Do you think this one continued to kill other people?" he asked her. "I mean, so often you do connect your cases to my cases," he noted, "and I never really understand how."

"Instinct," she replied.

"Which doesn't hold up in court."

"I know that, trust me," she said. "And it's one of the reasons why I struggle because I think people need to be better. I think they should be nicer to each other."

"Of course they should," he agreed, "but that doesn't mean they will be, at least not on your say-so."

She glared at him. "They should."

He grinned. "Yes, they absolutely should. But whoever did this … could also potentially be either very old, like Bernard Winters, or already dead. You need to prepare yourself for that."

"I know," she muttered, "but I don't want them to be dead. I want them brought to justice."

"So, you're assuming foul play was involved?"

She looked at him in surprise. "Do you really think it's possible it wasn't foul play?"

"Sure. He fell off a building and someone found him on the sidewalk, already dead. They buried him instead of reporting it. Yeah, not a great example, but all I'm saying is, you can't jump to conclusions."

"Why not?" she muttered. "It seems to me that is something people do all the time."

"Sure, but that doesn't make it right. That doesn't lead to the facts. And we need evidence."

She groaned. "I'll give you that."

When he was done documenting the current state of the crime scene and beyond, he looked around and nodded.

"Not a whole lot that can be done here, is there?" she asked, as she too looked around.

"No, not at this stage, but we must get everything we might need before we release it back to the city. I understand the park will be reopened to the public soon."

"Do you think anybody will care that someone was buried here?"

He nodded. "Plus, I wanted to see if anybody would come back to the scene of the crime, now that the crime scene tape is gone, and it's been opened up to the public again."

Her eyes widened with excitement, as she slowly nodded. "That is a really good point."

"Thank you," he replied, with a mock bow. "I would like to think I can be of service occasionally."

She smacked him lightly on the shoulder. "Oh, stop. You do an incredible job, and you know it. I'm the one who just blunders around in the dark and somehow manages to get people to either talk or to make a mistake."

"I think any unidentified criminals are all scared of you," he said.

She frowned, then nodded. "You could be right."

"Hey, I was joking," he replied, raising his hands in defense under her piercing gaze.

"No, I think you're right. I think they're scared of me because I delve into these cases and then won't let it go. So, then they're afraid of what I could find—or what I will find."

"That makes sense," he admitted. "The thing is, if you bring up fear in people, they tend to lash out."

"Exactly, and I'm not too bothered about them lashing out verbally. Sometimes I'm tempted to do a little more lashing out right back, especially if people will be jerks about it all."

He smiled. "I don't think they're necessarily being jerks. They're just following their instincts for self-preservation."

"I am on my way after them," she announced, "so, if they don't like it, they'll have to run."

He frowned at her and added, "Let's not announce that to the world. I really don't want you to get hurt."

She smiled. "I'm not planning on getting hurt."

"You might not plan on it," he noted, giving her a death stare, "but we both know how quickly the tide can turn. You've had an incredible amount of luck with solving these cold cases and with surviving people attacking you," he pointed out. "So, yes, by now, you've made a lot of really interesting deductions that ended up being correct, something that warrant a scientific study in itself," he murmured, followed by a headshake. "But the bottom line is that we don't always have answers—or the ability to keep you safe."

"Which is why I have the animals with me," she shared, with a sweet smile, then caught sight of an older couple, slowly walking through the park, holding hands.

Mack saw it too and smiled. "It's nice to see, isn't it?"

"It is very nice to see," she began. "But then again, based on what you were just saying about people returning to the crime scene—"

"Do you really think that old couple is somebody returning to the crime scene?" he asked, his eyebrows raised.

"Not necessarily," she conceded, with a headshake. "But

considering the estimated age of our victim, it certainly could be."

"Good point," he muttered. He put down his cup of coffee and said, "Wait here with the animals, please." With that, he strode off in the direction of the couple.

Chapter 7

D OREEN WATCHED AS the old couple stopped and talked with Mack for several minutes, before he walked back toward her. "And?" she asked him curiously.

"They've lived in the area a long time and had no idea a body was found here."

"When you say, a long time?"

He smiled and noted, "Forty-plus years."

"So, maybe not long enough."

"Maybe not," he conceded. "We need Elizabeth's report to help us determine that. On the other hand, I asked them if they knew of anybody extremely tall who may have gone missing. They looked at me in complete surprise and shook their heads. I did give them a card, just in case they remember something."

"And that'll be the trick to this, won't it?" she asked. "It's his height that might stick out. Nan even brought that up."

"At least it gives us something to focus on, short of identifying him," he pointed out. "Still, with possible witnesses of their age, memories may be problematic. So we'll have to do a whole lot more detective work before we have enough facts to trigger something specific, or to get anyone to care about something that happened so long ago."

"And how sad is that?" she muttered. "Everybody should care whether it's today or fifty years ago."

"We're still waiting for time of death confirmation too. We have to give Elizabeth time to do her job and to do it fully and completely to the best of her ability."

Doreen nodded. "I sure would like to have a few more answers than we have right now."

"I went to the hospital to talk to the X-ray department. They didn't have anything to say, except pointing me in the direction of somebody down in Vancouver who recycles the film."

"Interesting," she replied excitedly. "That could be a trigger for a lead. Could they read the X-ray?"

"Yes and no," he said, with a shrug.

"Which one is it? Yes or no?"

"The X-ray was quite damaged, but they found a series of blows that our exceptionally tall, very dead friend sustained. It was in the lower portion, hips and whatnot. Both femurs were broken, one kneecap appeared to be damaged, and the rest was a little fuzzy. They could guess at some of it, but no more than that."

"Both knees?"

"Both legs and one kneecap."

She grimaced, as she stared at him. "That sounds quite gang related."

He nodded at her. "Or mafia related, I would say."

"Right." She gave him an eye roll. "Same diff."

He laughed. "I don't think the mafia would consider themselves to be a gang under any circumstance," he clarified, with a laugh. "I'm pretty sure they consider themselves to be a cut above all that. *The family, the number one family of all.*"

"Maybe," she muttered. "But they're still just hoodlums to me."

"They are the spark of the old gangs, but they have slowly moved on. Even we don't know a lot about the mafia. We could talk to the old couple here and see if they recall any mafia presence in the area. They've certainly been around long enough for that."

She looked over at them, and Mugs stared at them too. "What do you think, Mugs? Do we need to keep talking to them?"

He gave a gentle *woof* in response.

She nodded. "Maybe I'll go over and talk to them myself," she suggested. When Mack frowned at her, she shrugged. "It just feels as if I should." She took the two leashed animals and veered off, leaving Thaddeus with Mack. Only that didn't last long. As soon as Thaddeus realized they were leaving without him, Doreen heard a flutter of wings and a squawk, as he raced along behind them. "And here I thought you just might want to stay with Mack a little bit," she said, waiting for him to catch up, which caught the attention of the old couple.

They stopped and looked at her in amazement.

Doreen smiled and said, "Hello."

"My goodness, are you that detective woman we've heard so much about?" the wife asked.

"I'm an amateur sleuth," she clarified. "He's the real detective." She pointed back to Mack, who had stayed behind and now appeared to be on his phone.

"Oh my," the wife replied.

"We've heard all about you," the old man grumbled.

Doreen laughed. "I don't know if that's a good thing or a bad thing," she replied, with a bright smile. "But I appreciate that you've had the chance to hear about me."

"Oh yes, oh yes," the wife declared, with a bright smile. Her husband didn't appear to be quite so enamored, which was fair enough. "What are you doing here now?" the wife asked, giving her a curious smile.

"Oh, just looking into this whole mess here," she replied, with a nod at the park.

"What mess?" the woman asked.

"How long have you lived near here?" Doreen asked. "Maybe you would know something."

"No, I told the detective I didn't know anything about it," the woman replied, with an airy wave of her hand. "I mean, it's not the kind of thing people like us would know about."

Doreen frowned at her in surprise. "There is no such thing as *people like us* in a case like this," Doreen declared. "It's simply a case where somebody lost his life and was buried here."

The woman winced. "Again, still not something that would apply to us," she repeated. "We've always kept to ourselves and avoided the trouble that comes from this area."

"And what trouble would that be?" Doreen asked curiously. "I didn't realize trouble was here."

"Oh my, yes," she stated. "I mean, I don't know what trouble it was, but you could always count on something going on."

"Oh, so it would make sense to you that somebody would have been buried here?"

"I don't know about that. Nothing makes sense to me when it comes to that," she replied, with a self-conscious laugh. "I don't even begin to think those kinds of thoughts."

"What did you do for work?" Doreen asked her curiously.

"I was a teacher."

"Oh, how interesting. Did you ever have a student who was super tall?"

"Had a couple of them over the years," she noted, "but I wouldn't know what became of any of them. It's not as if I stayed in touch or anything."

"How long were you teaching?"

"Thirty years," she stated proudly.

"Oh, that's lovely," Doreen noted, with a beaming smile in her direction. "That's beyond lovely. Gosh, you must have an awful lot of insider knowledge about what the kids were like and how Kelowna has changed over the years."

"Oh." The woman flushed. "I don't know anything about all that. I mean, I get that everybody wants to have information about what happens in this corner of the world, but it's just the same as anybody else's corner. I don't have any answers."

"No, of course not," Doreen said, with a nod. "And there isn't really any answer in a case like this, after all."

"Isn't there?" she asked, studying Doreen. "I thought that's what you do."

"It's what I try to do, but we're very early on in this case. So, I don't know that we'll get too many answers. It was a very long time ago."

"Was it?" the wife asked, looking back at the park, and then she gave a slight shiver. "I don't know how many times I've walked over that area."

"Right, that'll be something everybody thinks about now," Doreen pointed out. "How many times did you walk that area, and yet you didn't know?"

"None of us could have known," the wife declared. "The only one who would have known would be the killer."

"Exactly," Doreen agreed. "So, if that killer is still around or even still alive, we'll will find him eventually," she declared, with a note of authority in her tone.

"That's a big job," the old man finally spoke up again, "especially if it happened long ago."

"It probably was a long time ago, and you're right. It is a big job, but it bothers me to think of people getting away with this."

"Do you even know that it was murder?" the wife asked, adjusting the collar of her coat tighter to her neck. "Isn't it a little early for that?"

"Maybe," Doreen admitted, "but wouldn't you bury somebody properly, unless it was underhanded and criminal?"

"Maybe they didn't have the money," the wife suggested. "We've certainly known lots of very poor families in this town who didn't have money for things like that."

"Isn't there help for cases like that?" Doreen asked.

"Now, maybe—but back then? I doubt if there was. Back then there didn't appear to be help for anybody," the wife shared. "It's one of the hardships of teaching. You see so many people who could use help, and there just isn't anything available for them."

"You're right there," Doreen muttered. "That would break my heart."

"Aren't you a very wealthy woman now?" the old man growled. "It sounds as if you should be helping a lot of people financially."

Doreen raised her eyebrows. "I *might* end up as a very

wealthy woman eventually, but I certainly don't have any of it now. With all the legal business pending, I don't have the slightest idea of when it will all be completed or even how much it entails," she shared, with half a laugh. "However, helping others is definitely something I'll consider at that time."

The man just grumbled something under his breath, which didn't sound the least bit complimentary, so she let it slide.

Doreen nodded at the wife, who was eyeing her husband in concern. Doreen asked, "Presumably there are charities that handle that sort of thing these days?"

"I don't know if there are or not," the old woman replied, as she nudged her husband forward. "Good talking to you," she said, with a bright smile, as the woman quickly moved her husband away from Doreen.

Doreen watched them go, wondering at the man's attitude.

When the wife turned to look back at her, she frowned when she saw Doreen still staring at them and urged her husband away faster.

As Doreen slowly walked back to Mack, he pointed at the retreated couple and noted, "That didn't seem to go all that well."

"It's interesting because, while the old man wasn't friendly to begin with," she noted, "toward the end we were talking about the cost of a burial. He made a comment about me being a wealthy woman now and how I should be helping with burials, if people can't afford them."

Mack frowned at that, then looked back at the old couple, who were now just a shadow in the distance. "Interesting," he replied thoughtfully.

"That's what I thought," she murmured. "I'm not sure if he even knows who I am, or just thinks he does."

"As we all know," Mack began, turning to her, "everybody will have an opinion about what you may or may not have and about what you'll do with it. They will look at it through their own filters, prejudices, and life experiences, and somehow feel as if they are entitled to judge or to comment on what they think they know about your situation."

She nodded. "And I'm not saying he should or shouldn't do that. It was just interesting to see his take on it."

"Good enough," Mack said, with another glance at the old couple. "I'm ready to leave here and to head back to the office. Are you good to go?"

She nodded. "Good to go."

As they all got back into Mack's truck, she couldn't stop herself from looking around to see where the old couple may have disappeared to.

"You want to drive around and see where they went?" he asked.

She looked at him and muttered, "If I was alone, I would."

He changed directions and said, "Keep talking."

"Something was off about him."

"Doesn't make him a killer," Mack stated.

"No, it doesn't. However, it does make him somebody full of prejudice and anger about something, and he didn't have anything good to say. So, …"

"Still doesn't make him a killer," he pointed out.

"No, of course not," she murmured. "Just odd." As he went to open his mouth, she added, "I know. I know. *Still doesn't make him a killer.* Right age group though," she noted, with a smile. "You've got to admit that's an interesting point."

He smiled at her and stated, "The largest age demographic in Kelowna right now is those over sixty-five years old. Something like 31,000 or so."

When she heard that, she laughed. "I didn't think there were that many."

"These towns are aging quickly. An awful lot of long-term families are here, plus multigenerational families, who will have a lot more seniors than in other areas. Plus, we have all the retirement homes here, too, that pull in that age group."

"Which is another interesting concept," she replied, "but I'm not at all sure that it'll help us."

"No, if anything," he clarified, "it'll hinder us because there'll be so many, and we'll have a hard time even interviewing some of them, asking to see if anybody they knew went missing decades ago. Plus, you know that witnesses are not infallible, and then we have the age factor to consider."

As he drove around the block, Doreen watched up and down the streets to see where the old couple had gone. They had driven around several blocks, when she finally pointed. "There."

And there they were, the older couple, still moving at a steady pace toward their destination. When they turned into a small yard and walked up to the front door, Mack drove past, and Doreen took note of the address.

"You got a reason for that?" he asked, studying her curiously.

She shrugged. "Outside of the fact that something felt very wrong, no. But … something did feel wrong, so yes."

He smiled but didn't say anything.

"What's this?" she asked in a teasing tone. "You're interested in my crazy methods?"

"If you have a method," he said, "it would be interesting to know what it is. The trouble is, you don't have a method, as far as I can tell."

"No, maybe not," she acknowledged. "A lot of it is instinct."

"I get that," he said.

"And I know. I know," she replied, holding up her hand. "As far as you're concerned, it's all a load of malarkey."

He laughed. "No, that's not what I was going to say. What I would say is that it works for you. I just don't know that it would work for other people."

"That's because it's my system—if it is a system," she pointed out. "I mean, for you to go by instinct, I think you would have to fight with yourself the entire time. Whereas for me, it feels very natural." He didn't say anything, just nodded. "Besides, as you said yourself, I still have to have proof."

"Agreed," he said, with a wry smile. "But you do seem to get enough information that we end up getting the cases closed, regardless of how it makes anyone feel."

She smiled at him. "Hang on a second. Is that supposed to be a compliment?"

"Nope," he admitted, with a burst of laughter. "I was just curious. So, now you've got an address where they live."

"I do," she confirmed.

"Does it mean anything?"

"Maybe not."

But, as they drove past once more, Doreen looked over to see the old lady on the front steps, staring at them. Doreen smiled and waved. The old lady, a look of shock on her face, hurried inside and shut the door.

Doreen grimaced. "If they have done anything wrong, they're worried about it now."

"But that could just mean they didn't put the right thing in the recycling bin," he pointed out. "Some people get completely paranoid over nothing."

"Sure, and some people," she added, "get completely paranoid over things that they have done in the past that they're constantly waiting to get caught on."

"You think that's what this is?"

"Do I think that? No, I'm not sure what this is," she admitted. "All I can tell you is that it's something, but it may very well have nothing to do with our case."

"And, on that note," Mack said, "I'll take you home and head back to the office."

Chapter 8

DOREEN WASN'T SURE about Mack driving her around, just to see what she would do. However, she did admit it was nice to have him with her while she went looking for more info. It's not as if she sought something specific. She was seeking possibly anything that could be connected, and that made it different and harder to do. A whole huge city was here, and a lot of people had their own reasons for doing stuff. Mack was right about that. That couple in the park may have had absolutely nothing to do with the poor dead man case that she was working on. On the other hand, maybe they did, and at least this way she had an idea of who they were, even if it wasn't *what* they were. She was glad to have at least something to look into.

As she got home, she walked into the house with the animals and put on a cup of tea. She wanted very much to just sit down and think. Yet nothing really was coming to mind as to what she was supposed to think about. She needed to do a brain dump, and yet there wasn't a lot of information for her to do that yet.

She liked to do it when she had too much data, seeming-ly not connected, so she could better understand what was happening. She'd heard some people call it a brain-dump journaling. That made sense in that she was just jotting down those random tidbits on paper. And here she was, not even sure what thoughts she should be putting down. With a cup of tea at her side, she went ahead and wrote out the little bit that she had so far.

When Nan phoned, she asked, by way of a greeting, "And?"

"And what?" Doreen replied, her mind still on her notes.

"Did you find anything?"

"No, I haven't found anything yet. And we haven't heard anything from the coroner."

"Oh, dear," Nan muttered, disappointment in her voice. "How long does it take?"

"I don't know," she murmured. "Did you talk to Richie or anybody else about that park or that area of town?"

"I talked to several residents, but nobody knew anything about it. In fact, nobody had any recollection of anybody going missing, … particularly a very tall man going missing." she clarified, "which is always suspicious in itself."

Doreen laughed. "Maybe," she replied, "but a missing man who was very tall seems to make disappearing him all the more difficult."

"Right. Tall is not something you can easily fake or easily hide."

"No, I don't think so," Doreen agreed, but it was a question that she wanted to ponder a little more because that's all they really had in terms of helping with an ID. There were teeth in the partial jawbone, so they might get DNA from that. But still, they would need something to match it to. "Now that we've got some of the genealogy stuff happening more and more with the public sector, the police department might very well go ahead and utilize that too."

"I would think so. I mean, you did show them that it works."

"It wasn't even so much me," she pointed out. "Just the fact that cases all over the world are getting solved that way. Not everyone and not all the time but sometimes, and it still takes a very long time to get a hit because it requires somebody else to input matching DNA."

"Right," Nan muttered in a gloomy tone. "I could be dead before we solve this one."

Doreen burst out laughing. "And yet you might be doing just fine because it'll happen next week."

"I hope so," she declared indignantly. "An awful lot is riding on you."

"Oh no, please tell me you didn't set up a betting pool on this one."

"What do you mean, *on this one?*" she asked. "We set one up on every case, child. Of course we do. Everybody wants to know how you're doing."

"And what happens when I don't solve one?" she asked. "It's putting a lot of pressure on me too, you know?"

"Ah, if you don't solve it, you don't solve it. That's a given. It's not your fault. It's not as if they give you much to work with," she grumbled. "Some of these cases, I swear, you're just finding out the answers by sheer luck."

Doreen sighed. "Believe me that I'm very much aware of that."

Nan groaned. "I didn't mean it in an insulting way, so you can't take it that way."

"No, of course not," she replied, with a wry tone. "I just had an odd thought that maybe, just maybe, one of these days, I won't solve one of these cold cases, and everybody will feel … let down somehow."

"They can't feel let down by you. You've solved so many cases already. Surely everybody would give you a free pass on not being able to solve one out of so many."

Doreen winced. "Not sure that there is such a thing as a free pass on these cases."

"No, maybe not. I guess you'll just have to solve it, so you don't get a black mark on your record." And, with that, she added, "I've got to go. We're doing something down at the dang ballroom today." And she ended the call right away.

"Dang ballroom?" Doreen repeated out loud, as she put down her cell. "What on earth could they be doing in the dang ballroom?"

She smiled to herself, thinking about how very busy and active Nan's life was down at Rosemoor and how much fun she was having in her old age. Particularly at having found a group of cronies who were almost as much trouble as she was. With a smile, Doreen returned to her brain dump of notes. Deciding that maybe Solomon's files might have something to offer, and needing to refresh her memory anyway—just in case she ever thought she would miss something—she pulled out her index and slowly read through the summary entries she had made for each of Solomon's files.

Nothing really came to mind after the first read, but, as she went through her index of Solomon's files the second time, something there made her ponder.

Another person, a woman, had gone missing, and her body had been found … where? She looked at her notes, and all she saw was Rutland.

"Rutland," she repeated, "and a woman's body."

She thought about it for a long moment, wrote down as

much of the case number as she had, then phoned Elizabeth Harley.

When the coroner answered, she sounded a little testy, as she bypassed any greeting and stated, "I have no answers for you."

"You may not," Doreen noted, "and I wouldn't be at all surprised. I knew this would take some time. I may not like it, but I know how it is. However, there was a prior case, and I don't know if it's connected because I can't … of course, I can't get very many details of a woman who went missing a good fifty years ago. Yet her body was found in Rutland, about two years ago, I understand. Anyway," she said, "it was found under very similar circumstances, with the same type of burial."

"What case is this?" Elizabeth asked, almost affronted that she didn't know anything about it.

Doreen gave her the case number and suggested, "It's likely in the cold case files."

"I'll have to take a look," she replied, "but I'm not at all sure anything could be quite as similar to this."

"No, I'm not saying there is. It just seems … curious."

"No, you're right," Elizabeth muttered, her tone almost sliding into a far-off note. "Look. I am a bit occupied, but I'll get back to you." And, with that, she ended the call.

Doreen stared down at her phone, wondering just what she had triggered because it was obvious that something had popped up in Elizabeth's head. And that was a good thing because anything that triggered a response was always helpful. As she waited for the coroner to get back to her, Doreen was left sitting here. After an hour of staring down at her cell, Doreen groaned. It would drive her nuts just sitting here and waiting. When her phone did ring, it was Mack.

"Hey," he began, "I just got off the phone with Elizabeth, … Dr. Harley."

"*Right*." Doreen groaned inwardly. "I phoned her about a cold case earlier this morning."

After a moment of silence, he asked, "You did?"

"Yeah, I did, about a woman who was found in Rutland."

"She didn't mention that part."

"The bottom line is, I found a reference to it in Solomon's files. So, I called her, just in case any similarities popped up with it and our very tall missing man. She seemed almost, I don't know, affronted that she didn't know about it. She ended the call fairly quickly, as if something went off in her mind during our discussion."

"Yes, I would say so," Mack agreed. "And you're right. I want to come take a look at anything you've got in Solomon's files."

"Sure, but I can easily send you a copy."

"I'll come take a look at the originals." And, with that, he ended the call.

She frowned at her phone, then over at the animals sprawled all around her. "Well, boys, something is definitely up."

Chapter 9

DOREEN OPENED THE door for Mack with a smile on her face, which fell away almost immediately. "So, apparently my phone call to Elizabeth triggered something."

He nodded. "That it did, and not necessarily in a good way."

"I'm sorry. Did I do something wrong?" she asked, staring at him. "I just went to Solomon's files and thought that maybe something in there was about a tall man going missing. Instead a missing woman had been found, also in Rutland."

He smiled and nodded. "You haven't done anything wrong. Yet … you have triggered a case that has stumped people for a long time."

"Why isn't it already in your case files then?"

"It didn't pop up because she's already been found."

"And identified?"

"We thought she was, until the family did a DNA test recently, and it wasn't a match."

She stared at him. "You need to fill me in on that."

"We have a retired US senator, a dual national, both American and Canadian, who has spent a fair bit of time up here in Canada. His daughter came up to get away from the politics at the time. Anyway, she disappeared, and that was a long time ago. When we thought her body had been found, everything was wrapped up and closed out. Only, for whatever reason, the family decided to run a DNA test."

"So, run DNA on what?"

"The coroner kept samples from the autopsy, and the family apparently kept the ashes."

"But you can't run DNA off ashes. I've been told that, just because you've got ashes, it doesn't mean you've got the right ashes."

He stared at her for a long moment. "You are right about that. In this case, we had some samples from the autopsy of the dead female and compared it to a hair sample from the senator's daughter, which the mother kept in a locket. We found out recently that the bones they had claimed as their daughter wasn't their daughter."

Doreen blinked at him several times. "So, they had them cremated and had a ceremony to say goodbye to their daughter, only to find out it wasn't her? So, now we have ashes belonging to somebody, who we don't even know who they are, and the family again has a missing daughter?"

He nodded slowly. "That about sums it up, yes."

"Good God," she muttered. "Are the parents holding you guys liable?"

"They are the ones who claimed it was their daughter. We sent off dental records and a few other things, and they confirmed it was her."

She frowned at him. "So, you know what the answer here is."

"I know what people are saying is the answer, but the parents are denying it."

"Of course they are. It sounds to me as if maybe the mother tried to pass off another man's child as her husband's. Depending, of course, if the DNA matched the mother or father."

"And that is, of course, one of the suppositions we are working on."

"Good God." Doreen snorted. "There is no end to this confusion, is there?"

"No, there sure isn't," he murmured, as he walked toward her little office space, to the side of her kitchen. "Where are you keeping Solomon's files these days?"

"Over here." And she brought him to where the boxes of the original files were.

He brushed his hair back as he stared at the various boxes. "Do you have any idea where that file is?"

"Yep, I sure do." She pulled up the index on her phone and explained, "Remember how I went to all that work and indexed everything?"

He shrugged. "I remember you doing something, but I guess I didn't quite understand what."

"Yeah, well that *something*," she explained, with an eye roll, "was to sort these files into something that was usable, something that we could search using keywords. I think …" After checking her notes, she walked over, removed a couple boxes, and brought up the one box that she was interested in. "I think it's in here." They took the lid off, and she went through the files and pulled up the one they wanted.

She handed it to him, and he sat down on her living room floor and went through it carefully. He frowned. "You're right. It is this file. Interesting that it was open, per Solomon."

"Yes, because you had all just been informed that it's not

his daughter."

Mack nodded. "That is, of course, one of the issues. They have since done DNA on both parents, but we're waiting on results. So now the parents are trying to figure out just what's going on. In the meantime, they're actively looking for their daughter."

Doreen shook her head. "So, we found a tall man. We found someone's daughter, and now we're looking for another family's daughter."

He stared at her and nodded.

"*Great.* That's just the thing we need right now. Not to mention up here in this part of the world," she noted, "it's pretty remote, so a dead body could be anywhere."

"It is pretty remote, and any dead bodies could be anywhere," he admitted. "Keep in mind that burying the dead when they've been murdered is almost always in a space that's remote and not exactly used by many people."

"So how could it be connected to this poor man's body?" she asked, staring at him.

"It might not be. All I can tell you is that we don't know enough yet."

She frowned, then nodded. "In that case, we need to keep looking for a whole lot of things."

"We do," he agreed, with a smile. He asked her, "May I take this to get a copy? I'll give it right back."

She shook her head. "We'll just copy it right now."

"You really don't trust me?"

"No, I don't want to lose them, even if only for archival purposes."

"Archival purposes," he repeated, looking at her sideways as she got up, took the file over to her printer, turned on the copier and started scanning the pages.

"I went through the digital version of this," she shared, "but I think I would like to sit down with the original and reread it again."

He nodded. "You're really into preserving his work, aren't you?"

She shrugged. "I don't know if I'm into preserving Solomon's work as much as understanding it. All these cases are still not solved."

He stared at the boxes and shook his head. "I don't even know how many of these cases are in our files," he noted. "I keep forgetting you've got all these. And it's absolutely astronomical to consider that they are all unsolved cases."

"That's true. At least they were unsolved according to Solomon. What that meant to him though, I don't know."

Mack nodded. "That's another good point. Just because he had them in his unsolved files, that doesn't mean we have them as cold cases. Or, if they are, we could have solved them, and he might not have known to update his records."

"And," she added, "it doesn't mean that they were ever official police cases. Maybe people didn't come forward to you at the time, but chose to talk to Solomon instead."

He frowned as he stared at the boxes. "This collection of Solomon's cold cases alone could be a full-time job."

"I know," she murmured. "And any time I think I'll run out of cases to solve, I keep looking at the boxes and think, … no, I won't."

He smiled. "It was quite a responsibility he gave you."

"I don't think he gave me the responsibility. I think he was hoping that I would be interested in pursuing the responsibility," she clarified, with a glum look at the boxes around her. "It would obviously be nice if I could do something with all this and make all these unsolved files join that box over there." And she pointed off to the side to a large one.

"What's that box?"

She beamed. "Those are the ones that I have dealt with. Those are closed, solved, and don't belong in his mess of unsolved ones anymore."

He stared at the single box and then back at the other pile of boxes and shook his head.

"I know," she muttered. "It doesn't look as if I've done anything."

"Honest to God, what you've done is amazing. Absolutely amazing. Yes, what we have to do now is … focus on what's at hand before we go running off into other directions."

"I understand that, from your point of view, all of this is going off in other directions, but from my point of view …" He focused on her as she continued. "From my point of view, it could very well be connected. That's why I brought up the case to Elizabeth Harley."

"Yeah," he muttered, with a wry look. "I'll give you the benefit of the doubt because you did make the connection. Elizabeth's now all over it, and I'm sure she'll be singing your praises."

"I don't want singing praises. I just want to help solve the case." Just then her phone rang. She smiled at the Caller ID. "Hey, Elizabeth," she answered.

"Hey, I wanted to tell you something before I got too carried away. Regarding that tidbit you called me about, the missing woman? It twigged something in my mind, and I had to go check it out. Then I had to contact the captain about it."

"Of course," she noted, looking over at Mack. "I presume it was helpful?"

"It was very helpful. It's all a bit discombobulated, and I don't even know if I'm allowed to talk to you about it. So maybe have Mack fill you in on the details, but it's pretty fascinating stuff. Anyway, I wanted to tell you that you did great again, so thanks. Oops, there's my other phone. I've got to go." And, with that, she ended the call.

Mack smiled at her. "See? You did good."

"She did seem to be pretty excited about it too."

"Oh, I'm sure she is, and, if you think about it, your one cold case is three cold cases now, and one is fairly predominant in the news."

"Is it?" she asked, turning to him.

He nodded. "Yes, whether we like it or not, whenever somebody is of a prominent position, even if in the past, it becomes something that everybody wants to get a piece of." He smiled and gave her a big kiss. "And, now that you've given me a full copy, I'm heading back to work." He stopped at the front door and looked back at her. "What will you do?" he asked.

"I'll sit down and read Solomon's file from front to back," she shared.

"Good, so, when I get off duty tonight, I thought I'd grab some steaks and maybe we could barbecue."

"Oh, that sounds lovely," she said, with a bright smile.

"Then we can compare notes," he suggested, and, with that, he was gone.

Chapter 10

WHEN DOREEN WOKE the next morning, she had this odd sense that she had solved something in her sleep. Yet she couldn't quite remember what the heck it was. Not the problem nor the solution. Grumbling to herself, she got up, had a quick shower, then made her way downstairs to the kitchen and put on some coffee. If she did one thing automatically every morning, it was that. As she waited for the coffee to drip, she had to wonder if the problem she'd solved in her sleep had anything to do with her current cold case, now *cases*.

The thought that there were three missing persons, plus two bodies, which may or may not be one of those three, blew her away. And that was the problem. Not necessarily that three went missing, but maybe none of these were connected. That was the thing about these cases. There were all these rumblings but not necessarily any real evidence to link them. At least not yet. As she thought about it, the missing senator's daughter was the greatest concern because some other woman had been buried in her place. Did anybody care about that misidentified woman? So, that body had been cremated and was not the body of the missing senator's daughter, and now they had this man's body.

She had to wonder if there was any possible connection. It seemed a little dubious that there would be, but she'd certainly seen weirder things. As far as she was concerned, the fact that the one man's body was found about the same time as the misidentification of the senator's daughter had popped up at the same time meant something, right? But what? Doreen needed to get the physical details on the still-missing senator's daughter, as well as details about the body they had found. How did the misidentification occur?

Was that ID process logged into the case files, or would she have to ask permission to get that too? She groaned, hating being stymied at getting what she needed. They could also easily say this senator's daughter's case had nothing to do with her cold case and that she needed to butt out. Particularly if it remained a high-profile case.

Nan phoned her before Doreen even had her first cup of coffee poured.

"I haven't had coffee yet," she grumbled, "so you might want to call back."

Nan burst into laughter. "Even when you're grumbling, you're way too much of a marshmallow to be much of a threat."

"I am not," she cried out, for whatever reason completely insulted by that. "I'm dangerous." Nan giggled, which somehow coerced a smile from Doreen. "Okay, I might only be dangerous to the cup I'm holding," she muttered, "but I'm hardly to be discounted."

"You're not to be discounted at all, my dear. So, rumor has it …"

"Rumor has what?" Doreen asked cautiously.

"Richie asked Darren something about it last night, and

Darren slipped and gave away something he wasn't supposed to. Now he's in trouble—or thinks he's in trouble anyway—and says it's all your fault."

Doreen snorted. "Since I wasn't part of the conversation with either Darren or Richie, how is it that I'm to blame or in trouble? People just want to blame me."

"You're right, but you should know by now that you make a great fall guy."

"I don't," she snapped, but then she groaned. "And what was it that Darren shared that got him into trouble?"

"Something about a senator's daughter."

"Oh, that."

"What? You know about it?" Nan cried out, and, when Doreen kept quiet, Nan was beside herself. "And you didn't tell us?"

"Having just found out yesterday, and not sure if I had clearance to share this," she explained, "I wasn't going to say anything, not until I talked to Mack today."

"I don't know why you're not already married to that man," Nan grumbled. "What's wrong with you?" Doreen went very quiet again, and Nan apologized. "I know. I'm sorry."

"Are you though?" she asked, with a groan.

"Yes, I am. You get to make these calls on your own. I don't care."

"Yes, you do."

"It would make you less cranky if you just told us and got that off your chest," Nan suggested.

Doreen glared into the phone.

Nan chuckled. "You think I can't tell that you're glaring into the phone already?" Doreen gasped and Nan cackled. "See? You're such a marshmallow."

"I am not."

"You are too."

"Am not."

At that, Nan just laughed again. "Why don't you come down, and you can tell us all about it? We already know some of it, and we'll just make things worse until we find out the truth. Therefore, you might as well come down and give us a better idea. That way we'll know what's going on and don't have to make it up."

"I'm sure you've already heard about it," Doreen muttered. "This was a case that was solved already."

"Sounds as if it isn't solved though."

"It was, but now it's not."

"*Right*," Nan muttered. "That makes no sense."

"You're right. It's all a bit convoluted, but I will finish this coffee and then make my way down with the animals."

"Come for breakfast. Richie has already been down to the kitchen. As soon as he heard about what was going on, he figured you were coming."

"He doesn't need to collect breakfast for me," Doreen pointed out. "I can eat just fine here."

"Yes, … you can, but we will all enjoy it if you come down. So, you might as well plan to eat with us," she explained. "We'll expect you in twenty-five minutes." And, with that, she ended the call.

Doreen stared sourly at her phone, and then she called Mack.

"Everything okay?" he asked, already distracted and caught up in work.

"Maybe and maybe not. Apparently the Rosemoor gang has already heard about the senator's daughter."

"You told them?" he asked cautiously.

"No," she replied, "but somebody else apparently couldn't avoid his grandfather's direct questions. I guess you need to toughen up that boy a bit." Mack groaned. "Preferably before the Rosemoor gang starts causing trouble and getting really difficult," she added. "They've asked me to come down to fill them in."

"So, now you're asking me if you can do that?" he asked, amusement in his tone.

"Yeah. Something about these *engagement rules* I don't quite get. Everything seems to have changed."

"Nothing's changed," he said. "And, yes, go ahead, fill them in on the case, and see if anybody has anything to offer."

"What?" she asked. "Is this you suggesting that we might have something to offer?"

"Don't push it," he growled and ended the call.

She glared down at her phone, called him right back, and, as soon as he answered, she stated, "Everybody is hanging up on me lately. The least you guys could do is make me feel better by letting me hang up on you once in a while." With that, she proceeded to hang up on him.

Then she burst out laughing, got up, got dressed, and headed down to Nan's place. Rosemoor was hopping. By the time she got there, people were gathered in Nan's apartment. Already six—no, make that seven people, as the seventh one tottered in with a walker—and darned if they weren't all wearing their Sherlock hats. As usual Richie brought goodies, and everyone seemed to be enjoying them.

Meanwhile, her animals were moving from person to person, hoping someone would drop something. Doreen sighed. At least they were behaving. She looked at the newcomer, and Richie made introductions.

"This is Danny. He's been around since forever."

"Hi, Danny," she said.

He beamed at her and nodded a greeting, even as he floundered his way into the closest chair. "Good God," he muttered. "Those hallways are getting longer and longer."

She had to admit that his progress getting here had him puffing, pretty much out of energy.

Nan pointed a finger at him. "If you hadn't worn yourself out bowling with us this morning, you wouldn't be so tuckered out."

"I couldn't let you win everything, now could I?" he declared, glaring at her. "You get away with way too much around here."

She snorted. "I don't get away with half as much as I should," she muttered. "And that's only out of concern for my granddaughter."

Doreen frowned at her and asked, "What have I got to do with this?"

"Well," she began, "you're always in the back of my mind. I don't want to mess things up between you and Mack. So, if I get into too much trouble, then Mack'll get into trouble and might get angry with you."

Doreen stared at her, her jaw dropping. "Wow, I guess you really do want me to marry him, don't you?"

Immediately Nan nodded and so did the rest of them. "We do, indeed, and we want you to do it sooner than later. Most of us"—she had the audacity to look somber, but Doreen saw right through the façade—"won't even be here at the end of the year."

Doreen sighed, unfortunately realizing that was a possibility. Yet the look on Nan's face was infuriating.

Nan, seeing the cloudy expression on her granddaughter's face, turned back to the others and announced, "Let's get to this now, before nap time." Doreen checked her watch. "Yes, it is approaching nap time for some of us," Nan declared, eyeing Doreen severely. "So we need to sort out some of these issues."

"What do we have now?" Richie asked excitedly.

Nan looked at him hard and turned to her granddaughter. "Doreen, you have the floor. Please explain about the senator's daughter."

"It's a little confusing," she began, "so I can't really answer too many of your questions. All I can tell you is what I have heard so far." And with that, she proceeded to explain the little bit that Mack had told her.

"Oh my," Maisie muttered, staring at her in shock.

"I know. It's one of those things where you can't quite believe it happened."

"You really can't, can you?" she added, as they all frowned at each other. "That's terrible that they buried somebody else's daughter."

"Yes, and it's also terrible," Doreen pointed out, "that another family doesn't know about their daughter."

"Oh my, yes," they cried out, almost as one.

"So, we have a couple big issues here," Doreen said.

Immediately they all straightened up to listen to her.

She sighed. "First, we need to know what happened to the senator's daughter. We need to know who was buried in that lavish ceremony, and we can't forget that we have an over-six-foot-tall male body that was just found in Rutland."

"Ooh," the newcomer, Danny, added, staring at her. "I don't know if you can handle all of these at once."

"We'll take them one at a time," Doreen replied in a reassuring tone. "And we'll probably find that they all dovetail into being connected."

At that, everybody asked, "How?"

"Think about it," Doreen replied. "How many times do we get that many different cases that aren't connected?"

"That's true." Nan nodded. "Yet this is definitely not our norm."

"Nope, it's not," Doreen agreed, "but I won't get fazed by it."

"Of course not," Nan declared, with a nod. "You've got way-too-much experience in this now."

"I don't know about having enough experience, but we do have a crisis here because the department will also be put on the spot now. They have to find the senator's missing daughter—the one case that everybody thought was already solved. And, of course, we still have to solve our current case involving the very tall man. Plus, we need to know the identity of the missing woman who was cremated by mistake by the senator and his wife."

"I think that's the part that hurts me the most," Maisie shared. "To think that somebody lost a child, and somebody else buried it as their own."

"It definitely won't be easy. On the other hand, we can't let it be something that really ruins this. We'll just take it one step at a time and be careful."

"In the meantime, does anybody remember anything about this senator's daughter's case?" Nan asked.

Danny nodded. "I think that's why Richie brought me over here," he suggested. "Back then, I was working as a newspaper reporter."

Doreen gazed at him with interest, as he preened in front of her. "You remember anything?" she asked.

"I remember that case quite well. However, nothing really came of the investigation. She went missing, and nobody had any idea where she was. I guess she'd gone to a party somewhere local. Various people stated she'd gone into the water, while other people were certain that she had taken off, but nobody knew for sure, and she was never seen again. It stayed in the public eye for quite a while, just because of who she was, being a senator's daughter, and then after that, ... it just got buried with other news, as it so often does."

Doreen nodded. "They do. It's hard to keep the momentum when working on cases where nothing is there to work with."

"Exactly," Danny confirmed. "We had our orders at the paper too. Everybody was to stay on it as much as we could, and then it got to the point where there was just ... nothing else to report. What do you say, except there's been *no new development?*" Danny shrugged. "You can only say that so many times before that phrase takes on the meaning of, *Hey, we failed.* So, everybody dropped it, hoping that something would come out of it eventually. Unfortunately, so far, there has been nothing to report."

Doreen nodded. "So, do we know who was with her at the time she went missing?"

Danny shook his head. "Nobody saw her leave."

"*Somebody* saw her leave," Doreen noted, with a groan. "But it's been so many years, it's hard to find witnesses that have something to say."

"I know, and that's part of the problem," Danny replied.

"What about the people who were partying with her? Were they all interviewed?"

"Oh my, yes. I'm sure many of them would say that we hounded them. I mean, obviously, if anybody knew anything, it should be them. So, they had both the police and the media after them for details."

"In theory, yes," Doreen conceded, "but I presume nothing came out of it?"

"No, nothing came of it, and then somebody found this body." Danny frowned. "I do remember hearing about that. It was maybe … a year or two ago. It was identified as the senator's daughter, and everyone cheered because another cold case had been solved and was done. And now they're saying it's not her."

"That's one of the questions I had for Mack. Is it that it wasn't her or is it that the father realized he's not the biological father of this daughter? So, my instinctive thought," Doreen began, looking around the room, "was that her mom had an affair and didn't tell her dad, then brushed the child off as his. That has certainly been done more than a few times back then."

"Absolutely," Nan agreed.

"However, because of the samples the coroner still had, they were able to be tested. That has proven that it's also not the mother's DNA either. Thus, everybody is now sure that it's not their daughter. So, of course, everybody is outraged."

"But did the parents not identify her?" Richie asked.

"They did. Supposedly the remains were identified as her."

Nan suggested, "So most probably she had some stuff on her, jewelry or something that belonged to the senator's daughter. I mean, there had to be something to connect this found body with the senator's daughter."

Doreen shook her head. "It wasn't that. Mack mentioned something about teeth."

The journalist stared at her. "That doesn't add up. Teeth should have been definitive."

"Should have been, ... yes, but now the questions I have are, who ID'd the teeth? Did anybody follow up and check the report, or did the dentist just say it was her? Could we be looking at a scenario where somebody got paid to say it was her?" When they stared at Doreen, she shrugged. "It must be devastating to have no answers for so long. I'm sure these parents want closure so badly that it may be a relief to believe that a body might be their child and the end of their search."

The journalist looked at her and slowly nodded. "Unfortunately that is very true. I mean, I would hate to see that in this instance, but we do know that it happens."

Richie asked, "What if the mom is the one who didn't want the DNA tested and was absolutely positive it was her daughter, and that was the end of it?"

"Sure, but then what?" Nan asked. "Was she the one who had the change of heart and wanted the DNA tested, or was it something else? *Someone* else?"

"I don't know," Doreen replied. "Those are all good questions, and we'll have to work our way toward getting answers. But that still doesn't change the fact that we need to know the real identity of this body, and we still need to know where the senator's real daughter is."

Chapter 11

AFTER SHE GOT back home from Nan's, Doreen sat down at her kitchen table and reviewed Solomon's files a little more carefully to see if she had missed or forgotten about yet another file. There were so many, far too many to remember, but she had that inkling of something in the back of her mind. As she worked her way through the summary that she had done, slowly reading, trying to figure out if any other cases would fit, she came across a woman named Sandy.

Doreen pondered it, pulled the file, then sat down and read it from start to finish. It wasn't very big but concerned a young woman named Sandy Wayne. Solomon had spoken to the family. They were from Vancouver, and the daughter had come up for a visit. She had also mentioned that she would go see some friends and family in Manitoba. Apparently she never arrived. The family wasn't sure if she went that far or if she changed her plans. They'd searched long and hard but found nothing.

Doreen stared at that for a long moment and then scanned it in and sent digital copies to both Elizabeth and Mack, texting, **We should test the DNA of the body now**

ID'd as *not* the senator's daughter against this case.

Almost immediately her phone rang. It was Elizabeth.

"Where did you get that from?" she cried out.

Doreen realized that Elizabeth probably didn't know about Solomon and his research files, so Doreen gave the coroner a basic rundown and added, "I just went through the files, looking for a potential match."

"I can't believe somebody just gave you all those files."

"It was his life's work," she explained. "He didn't want it to be forgotten, and he didn't want anybody thinking that all these people weren't worth looking into," she shared. "So, I made a promise to honor his work and to go through as much of it as I can."

"That in itself is quite a life's quest."

"I know, much to Mack's dismay, I'm sure."

She laughed at that. "Good to know that you're engaged to him, since it would be hard for the two of you to keep secrets from each other."

"I do try to honor the very blurry lines between us," she acknowledged. "And, yes, I absolutely cross them all the time."

"I'm sure you cross them sometimes, but not so much because you're not worried about it, but because you feel that you need to."

"Exactly," Doreen confirmed. "I think Mack understands that. If I cross these lines, he at least understands why I'm doing it and then maybe finds it easier to accept."

"Maybe, although I can't say I would take it very kindly if you got involved in any of my cases," Elizabeth Harley stated, almost with a note of warning.

"And I wouldn't," Doreen replied. "I mean, I can only pass over information and hope that people pick it up and move with it."

"I will take a look at this one," she said, "and see if there's anything to pursue."

"I do have Solomon's file on the woman who was identified as the senator's daughter," she added, "and they are definitely about the right age."

"Good, and that would explain why this case was never triggered because, as far as everybody was concerned, the other body belonged to the senator's daughter."

"Exactly," Doreen confirmed.

"Will you tell Mack about this one?"

"Yes, I already sent him a copy of the file."

"Good," she replied distractedly. "Then I will get to work on it right now." And, with that, she ended the call.

Moments later, Mack called. "Don't tell me. More from Solomon's files?"

"Yep," she replied. "One of Solomon's files and another family who's still looking for their daughter."

"Which in this case never got checked," Mack pointed out, "because the body had already been identified as somebody else."

"Exactly," she said. "And I can't guarantee that the body is Sandy's either."

"No, but it is a good guess," he noted, "and we appreciate it."

She frowned at her phone. "You're being awfully nice these days."

After a moment of silence, he asked, "Am I often not nice?"

"Sometimes, yes," she stated, with a laugh. "I'm used to that Mack."

He laughed. "Do you want me to go back to being *not*

nice? Not that I ever thought I was not nice, by the way."

"You weren't this polite. You weren't this … it feels as if you're being careful."

"And is careful not good?" he asked.

"Sometimes, no. Sometimes it feels … *off* maybe?"

He laughed. "I think you worry too much."

"Maybe," she muttered. "And, if I do, I know who to blame." Mack chortled, and she ended the call herself.

She also wasn't sure if the police had the budget for all these cases with DNA testing and whatnot involved. She didn't even know how that worked. If they had cases, did they have to deal with them? Could they turn them down, deciding they didn't have any budget money to investigate further?

It seemed as if that would be completely wrong, and yet quite possible at times that they would have no options when it came to budget money. None of these tests were cheap. She didn't know how expensive DNA testing was, but it was something that she could see herself getting behind. Particularly if a rape case were going dusty on the shelves. She pondered that and was still pondering it when her attorney, Nick, called. "Hey," she greeted him in a distracted tone.

He asked, "What's going on?"

"Do you know if a lot of untested rape kits are in town?"

There was silence on the other end of the phone for a moment. "I'm … not sure. How did we get on this topic? What's bothering you?"

"It's not so much that something is bothering me," she replied in frustration. "Well, yeah, obviously it is. We're currently working on a mix of cases, and I was thinking about how the budget seems to affect everything. Then I started worrying whether rape cases weren't solved simply because no budget money was allocated to run the kits and …"

"Hey, hey, easy," Nick responded. "You need to pace yourself. Remember that we can't solve everything in the world."

"I know," she muttered, taking a deep breath. "But a lot of money is coming my way, right?"

"Yes," he agreed, "a lot of money is coming your way."

"So, I don't know how this works because I've never had any money. However, if I invested some of it—enough for me and the animals to live on, plus some extra for emergencies or whatnot—could I put some into getting these DNA kits tested?"

He responded, his words filled with warmth, "I'm pretty sure nobody would have a problem with you doing that."

"Are you sure?" she asked anxiously. "Everybody tends to get upset with me when I step on toes."

"They might get upset at you for stepping on toes, but I don't think anybody will get upset for you wanting to help," he clarified. "And, of course, we could set up something, and we'll also need to get you set up with a financial adviser."

"Or two or three," she muttered, "like from different companies, to confirm nobody in the mix wants to cheat or to rip me off."

"That's not a bad idea," he agreed. "We can get multiple advisors and have them on one team, and they all would have to agree on what to do with the money."

"And the payouts for them is smaller," she added, "although I don't think they would agree to that."

"We'll explain right up front that they'll be on a consultation fee basis and won't get a percentage."

"A percentage," she repeated, aghast. "They're supposed

to get a percentage of the money?"

He laughed. "In most cases, yes," he confirmed, "but, for financial advisers, we can set it up however you want to set it up."

"I don't want them to get a percentage."

"But you've got to consider the idea behind that is, if they do get a percentage, then they'll work harder to make good investment decisions, so that their percentage is higher."

"Yes," she conceded, "I guess there is that point. But then if the percentage is higher, they still get more. So how will I help people if everybody's trying to take a chunk?"

"Let's get the money, get you investing, see what dollar figures you're looking at, and then you can think of helping others."

"I don't know if it's even a viable idea because I don't even know what it costs to do a DNA test," she noted, with regret. "How sad is that?"

"I doubt if anybody knows the cost to run DNA, except people in the field," he pointed out. "Stop knocking yourself down for not knowing things. Just call one of the local labs and ask them. Then we can figure out what's the best way forward, if that's something you want to do."

"It is something I want to do," she declared. "Obviously I need to know how many I can help. It might only be a few."

"I don't think it's that bad," he noted, "but again we'll figure it out."

She smiled. "Thank you for that."

"For what?" he asked, with a chuckle. "For stopping you from going off on a tangent?"

"No, I do that anyway. Just for the … the common

sense involved."

"You can also talk to Mack about it. Remember that."

"I know. I know," she muttered. "Just, … until it's set up, I don't want to tell people what I might do, especially if it turns out to be something I can't pull off. You know the finances more than I do."

He laughed. "I do know that there will be an awful lot of money and that you'll be a very wealthy woman. You were talking about doing some charities too."

"Right," she agreed, "so that's got to be taken into account."

"There's a lot of money, enough for several charities."

"Is there?" she asked anxiously. "And this will sound absolutely awful, and I don't even know that I want to think about what I'm saying right now, but I need to confirm I don't end up on the street."

"You will *not* end up on the street."

"Are you sure?" she asked, all bothered and anxious. "I want to help others, but I still have to live my life."

"Exactly," he confirmed, "so we give away an amount that you're comfortable with, and we will confirm that you have lots left over afterward. I don't think you have any idea how far the money you have will go."

"Of course not," she declared. "I didn't have anything to do with any of the money. Besides, one million dollars doesn't sound like a lot of money these days."

"Doesn't it?" he asked.

"Not really, but then I don't know what you do with one million. I just need a little bit for gas and the utilities and some groceries."

"Is that it?" he asked, with a note of amusement. "Are you planning a big wedding or a small wedding?"

"Small," she replied.

"Yeah? Are you sure? What about all the people who probably want to attend?"

She winced. "Mack mentioned something about that. I don't know what that means."

He added, "Anybody who you've had anything to do with will quite likely want to be there."

"Oh, ouch, that's a lot of people."

"It is a lot of people."

"Well then," she replied, "why don't we open it up and see if the city will let us have it down at the park, maybe down at the city center, and … can we do a picnic?" she asked. Then she stopped and frowned. "Except I told Mack *fourth quarter*."

"You told Mack fourth quarter for what?" he asked.

"I told him we'll talk wedding for the fourth quarter of the year. But then everybody seems to think—at least those at Rosemoor—that they won't even be around for this year's fourth quarter. So I'm starting to feel as if I need to have it earlier."

He burst out laughing. "Don't let anybody get to you," he suggested. "You do you in the time frame that works for you."

"You do know that if *you* were to get married," she shared in a persuasive tone, "it would let me off the hook. At least with your mother."

"No, no, no, that's not how it works," he said, through his laughter. "Because you getting married to my brother is getting me off the hook, remember? And that is something I really appreciate."

"In which case, you'll help Mack arrange everything without me, right?"

"Without you?" he asked, startled.

"I'm starting to think I'll get cold feet on the whole thing."

"Don't do that," he muttered, his tone serious. "You'll break Mack's heart."

"No, I wouldn't say no to him," she replied quickly. "But this whole wedding thing … just has Mathew vibes all over the place."

"That is a memory you need to get rid of," he pointed out, "because this has got nothing to do with your ex. If anything, you should be grateful for everything that's happened because now you'll help get some of these DNA kits tested, you'll help your favorite charities, you will help other people in general. If it had gone any other way, you could be the one needing charity. And thankfully it's not that way."

She smiled hearing that.

Nick added, "And, by the way, the reason I'm calling is that I do need some more paperwork signed."

She groaned. "Does that ever end?"

"No, it's just a fact of life. And it'll be a fact of your life for a very long time. So, just sign the paperwork and send it back."

"And what am I signing this time?" she muttered.

"To get the appraisals on all the jewelry and the paintings."

"Oh, did you contact Scott at Christie's?"

"I did, indeed, and he's thrilled. Believe me that he's *very* thrilled and that he's hoping to come down to go through Mathew's houses. So I'll go with him and take a look."

"Oh, good. Have him contact me afterward, will you?"

"Will do," he said cheerfully. And, with that, he ended

the call.

Doreen got an email from Scott not very long afterward, thanking her for considering him. When her phone rang, and she realized it was him, she smiled and answered it. "Who else would I ask to help me out of this bind?" she asked.

"And only you would consider it a *bind*," he stated, with a smile in his tone. "Apparently quite a bit of items are involved."

"My ex-husband was a bit of a hoarder, although he would say *collector*," she admitted. "And I'll probably have to make a trip down to the main house before we're done there because he had some … he had some secret hiding places. I'll have to think about those."

"Let me get a first go-through," he suggested, "because it seems there's a lot."

"There is a lot," she confirmed, "and I don't even know how many houses total, three or four I guess. I don't know if Nick's ready to appraise all of them or not."

"Wow," Scott replied, almost in a daze. "I guess that's what happens when things change hands, and everything has to be sorted."

"There is a list for insurance purposes somewhere. I do remember that."

"And we are contacting the insurance companies about it, but we can't always take the insurance company's values."

"No, of course not," she muttered.

"Now are you quite sure you don't want to see it all?" he asked. "Maybe you want to keep something for sentimental value."

She stared down at her phone, her stomach twisting at the thought. "No, I don't have happy thoughts regarding my marriage. Plus, I'm not the sentimental type. I would much rather sell it all off and use the money to pay for a whole province to clear the backlog of DNA rape kits sitting on the shelf untested, rather than keeping a piece for *sentimental value*."

After a moment of silence on the other end, Scott shared, "That sounds wonderful and makes me very happy to hear your plans. Now I'll make arrangements with your soon-to-be brother-in-law," he added. "If you do need to come down, it probably wouldn't be a bad idea."

"But it won't be any time in this next week or two," she pointed out. "I really don't want to travel when the weather is ugly."

"That's fine," Scott replied. "There's not any real rush, but, of course, there is always a rush."

"There's always a rush," she repeated, a smile in her tone, "but I understand what you're saying."

"Good," he murmured. "In that case, I'll leave you to it."

And, with that, she phoned Nick back.

"Miss me already, *huh*?" he teased.

She laughed. "I forgot to tell you this, but, in one house for sure—though I don't know about the others—but in the one house, he had some secret hiding places." Dead silence came from the other end for a long moment.

"And when you say secret hiding places, any idea what he hid in there?"

"No," she replied, not having a clue at all. "I don't. But I am pretty sure that, whatever it is, it's very valuable."

"*Great*. Do you remember where they are?"

"*Um*, kind of, … but they're a little hard to explain."

He added, "That just means you'll have to do a road

trip."

"Yeah, it does," she conceded, "but I want Mack to come with me."

"Good," Nick stated, "I'm not against that. We'll just have to figure out a time that works for all of us."

"Not just yet though, and we'll have to get Mack to book a day or two off work, which will be a challenge."

He laughed. "It will be, but, if you tell him what you want him for, I'm sure he'll make every effort he can."

And, with that, he ended the call.

Chapter 12

DOREEN WATCHED AS Mack stopped in later that evening, crashing down on a kitchen chair, sharing hugs and snuggles with the animals. She wasn't sure who needed that bit of sharing the most, Mack or her pets. She asked, "Is this a good time or a bad time?"

His eyebrows shot up. "It depends on what the issue is." She explained, and he just stared at her. "Secret hiding places, *huh*? I guess that makes sense, considering it's Mathew."

"It does and it doesn't. I just don't know about all of them. I did know of a couple rooms that he mentioned had them. Of course, his bodyguard would have something to say about us entering them, but I'm hoping that the properties are well and truly locked down, and nobody else can get in there."

On that note, he quickly pulled out his phone and started texting.

"I presume you're talking to Nick."

"I am, indeed, because this is something that would have been nice to have known earlier on."

"I'm sorry. I only remembered it as I was talking to Scott today."

His eyebrows shot up. "Scott? At Christie's?"

"Yeah, because he'll do an appraisal on a bunch of the artwork."

He nodded slowly. "I guess it's all expensive stuff, *huh?*"

She nodded. "Yeah, it really is. And I know Mathew was pretty stoked about having a lot of it."

"And you weren't?"

"They're just things," she muttered, "and really not my kind of things."

When she hesitated, he shook his head. "Okay, you need to come clean. Something else is bugging you."

She chuckled. "It's not that it's bugging me. It's just …"

"That means it's bugging you," he stated, with a nod. "Carry on."

"Well," she began, taking a deep breath, "it was something that came up earlier. Remember when we were talking to the grouchy old man in the park, and he mentioned something to me about having money and how I should do something with it?"

"Sure, and you were already planning on doing something with it," he pointed out. "You just haven't gotten the money and worked through the whole process yet."

"Exactly," she said, "and I don't know if this is a good idea or a bad idea." Then she hesitated again.

"I won't know if you don't spit it out."

"Okay. It bothers me to think that rape kits haven't been analyzed." He studied her, waiting, and she continued. "I don't know what we're talking about as to the cost to process each one or if there's a way to potentially donate money to get that done. Or if I need to set up … a foundation or a trust or something. Then maybe we could work on getting that backlog done."

She watched as a huge and incredibly gentle smile crossed his face, and he nodded. "That would be a lovely idea."

"Do you think so?" she asked anxiously. "Is it something that I can even help with? I don't even know what that would cost or what I eventually will get from Nick, when he distributes Mathew's estate to me."

"Any help would be great," he added. "I mean obviously we'd have to figure out how, and I don't even know what the backlog looks like for those rape kits." He took a moment and shook his head. "There is definitely some backlog."

"You hear all these horror stories from down south."

"Yes, and I don't think our backlog is as bad, but I really don't want to say that for sure."

"No, of course not," she noted, "and the minute we think it's not bad, we'll find out that there are all these cold cases that haven't been solved."

"I expected you wanted to put time and energy and money into the cold cases."

She grinned at him. "Oh, I do," she exclaimed. "I really do. However, I was hoping that maybe I could work on the cold cases a little more formally."

His eyebrows shot up. "We'll talk to the captain about that. I'm sure there are some legalities, but ..."

"But," she interjected, "money opens doors."

He grinned. "It opens doors, but also an awful lot of people could use a hand."

"I know, and I'm starting to make a list, which is hard since I don't really know how many I can help," she explained, "because that's still all in the realm of mystery, until the money is sorted."

"Of course it is," he agreed, smiling at her, "but the fact

is, I'm really proud of you for this. You are starting to get a good idea of who you want to help and how you want to help—and that's just as important."

"I feel as if there won't be enough money," she shared soulfully.

He smirked, shaking his head. "Maybe not, because, if you get too expansive on who and how you want to help, you can run through it pretty fast. However, if you invest it, so that a certain amount is designated to hand out every year, and you stick to that allotment, it can work. Not to mention you have or are getting tens of millions just from Nan's stuff, right? Mathew's and Robin's estates will double, triple that, I would assume."

"I hope it can. I talked to Nick about it."

"Good idea. I think you should work on setting up your own charity, designating certain sums to these other charities or projects or whatnot. Nick can probably help you with that too," he suggested. "I'm sure you can get way more done than you thought you could. Yet, even without knowing what kind of money is involved, at least you have an idea of where you want to start giving some of it."

She smiled. "You don't think it's a silly idea?"

He tugged her into his arms. "No, it's definitely not a silly idea. As somebody who works in law enforcement, I think it's an absolutely wonderful idea. And it makes me very proud that you've been thinking of it."

"Let's hope that we can do something about those rape kits," she declared. "As for Mathew's properties, I do know that there are those darn secret rooms. What I don't know is the extent of what might be in them."

"If you want to go treasure hunting," he offered, "I'm totally up for one."

She grinned at him. "That could be a lot of fun."

"We can meet my brother there too, assuming he's up for it."

"If you can leave your mother alone," she pointed out.

He stopped, considered that, and asked, "We'll probably be gone for what? … A weekend?"

"That was my thought," she said.

"Do you want to stay in the house?"

"Oh, I can't do that, can I?" Then she frowned.

He shrugged. "It's your house."

"Ooh, ouch," she muttered, rubbing her temples. "Let me think about it," she murmured.

"No pressure, but it is something to keep in mind."

"It is. I just hadn't …"

"I know." He smiled. "Of course you hadn't. It's not in you to really consider that."

"No, it's such a weird thing to even contemplate that, … that part of my life again."

"And it's one of the reasons Nick is doing all that paperwork, so we can get it out of your life," Mack pointed out, with a bright smile.

"Also something I hadn't really considered," she acknowledged. With a shake of her head, she asked, "Anything new on the cases?"

"No, nothing yet, and that's definitely troublesome."

"So, no new information on the X-ray films?"

"We've sent out images of them to the recycling company. So far, we haven't heard back. I did try to phone them this afternoon, but apparently some big convention or something is going on. The person I need to talk to about the old X-ray wasn't in the office, but he should be back tomorrow."

"Don't you just love that?" she muttered.

"Nope, I sure don't," he declared, with smile. "And I already know you don't."

"We want to know stuff."

"Right. And I often want to know stuff," he confirmed, as he eyed her intently. "I don't always get what I want either."

She glared at him. "So, you're talking about me not sharing everything with you."

"I'm happy to hear that you are sharing some things with me," he began, with a smirk. "But you and I both know that lots of times you try to skirt around sharing, so you don't have to tell me."

"Only if I think you'll take me off the case," she muttered. The grin that flashed across his face just made her heart melt even more.

"And I realize that," he acknowledged. "I know that you're doing everything you can do to help close these cases, and you have done more than a crazily phenomenal job. Yet we do need information on our time frame and not just your time frame."

She winced and nodded. "I get that. Hopefully, in this case, we can get some information and move forward."

"What? You don't have a way forward right now?" She glared at him, and he laughed. "How about a walk?" he suggested. "Just down the river and maybe get some fresh air. You seem to be struggling."

"I'm not struggling as much as … frustrated."

"Same diff," he said. "You and I both know that getting up and getting out for even a few minutes of fresh air often makes a huge difference—even if it is frigid fresh air."

Since he was absolutely right, she didn't bother arguing.

"I know the animals would be more than happy to have some fresh air too," she murmured. They got up, quickly put on jackets, deciding to forego all the leashes since they were right at their own home base.

She stepped outside, and the cold hit her in the face, and she gasped, the air sending icicles down to her lungs. "Wow, it got cold." Meanwhile, Mugs and Goliath ran outside, not deterred one bit. Thaddeus did snuggle closer to the warmth of her neck, hidden behind her hair. Doreen hoped he was cozy enough.

"It did get cold," Mack agreed, "and that is also to be expected. It is winter in Canada."

"Right. I'm still more accustomed to Vancouver-type weather."

"You can be accustomed to it all you want, but you're here now. Besides I'll take the cold over wet any day."

She glanced over at him and nodded. "So do I. Not to worry. I'm staying."

The briefest of smiles touched his face, and he grabbed her hand, and, holding hands, they walked down the river.

"Do you ever worry about me leaving?" It was a new thought, but now that it was in her brain ...

"No, but when you make comments sometimes, about it's really cold, it does concern me."

"*Nah*, you don't need to be concerned. I mean, the house is warm. Now, if I couldn't keep the house warm, that might be a different story."

"But you are not that same broke person anymore," he pointed out. "You probably have more money sitting in your bank account than you even know what to do with right now."

"I haven't checked," she muttered. "I was thinking about

picking up some Chinese food earlier today, and then had to stop and wonder if I had the money."

That set him off in peals of laughter.

She glared at him, and it took him a few minutes to stop laughing. She stormed ahead but couldn't get far as he wouldn't let go of her hand. "It's really not that funny."

"Yes, it really is from my viewpoint. It's hilarious, but I get it. You have to settle into realizing you have money, realizing you can certainly afford to go out and to get yourself something."

Doreen watched as Mugs headed right for the creek. "Don't get wet, Mugs. That creek water will be too cold."

Mugs turned to give her a quick look. Then he promptly put one paw in the water. Immediately he withdrew his paw and shook off the water. Doreen just sighed. "Pets are like kids who never grow up."

Mack stared at the long winter coat she wore and asked, "Where did you get that coat?"

"It's one of Nan's." His eyebrows shot up, and she nodded. "It's one of the pieces I kept when I did that massive culling out and cleaning of her closets. It's really nice."

"It is nice. It just blew me away when you said it was Nan's."

"It's a style that's come and gone and come all the way back around again," she noted, chuckling. "It's made of quality material."

"What is it made of?"

"Thankfully not fur, not my style at all. This is made of wool. And I really like it."

"It's an interesting rust color."

"I like that too."

As they walked, their talk turned around to the case. "I

did tell the group down at Nan's," she shared, "and everybody was pretty stumped as to what was going on, considering that we have three bodies now."

"Three?" he repeated, looking at her in confusion.

"We've got the body we just found of the very tall man."

"Right."

"We've got the body buried under the wrong name."

"Correct," he replied.

"And then there's the missing senator's daughter, who was never found."

"Right, but we have no body there."

"True. We have to find that body and to identify the other two."

"And you did contact Elizabeth."

"Yes, I did," she confirmed. "I mentioned the other missing woman's case from Solomon's files. Her name is Sandy Wayne. I think that could be a good match for who was misidentified as the senator's daughter. And hopefully something can be done with the DNA."

"That would be good," he replied. "It seems to have really set people off to consider that the wrong woman was buried under somebody else's name."

"Of course," she murmured. "When you think about it, that's everybody's worst nightmare. They're sitting around, hoping their missing child is found. However, it's been buried as somebody else's child. I just can't imagine."

"Of course not, and, along with everything else, it's very traumatizing for the senator's family as well."

"I know. Still a little odd that they would have thought it was their daughter to begin with."

"No, not necessarily," he explained. "I mean, they're already traumatized. Not a whole lot to see with a badly decomposed body, and they want it to be their daughter. Per the autopsy, the basic physical description fits. Then the teeth were supposedly a match, so it just seemed to be a slam dunk. They are so relieved that they have finally found her, and, even though it's bad news, it's still an opportunity to find closure."

She nodded, thinking about it. "I guess I hadn't really thought about it from that point of view," she murmured. "It's pretty rough for everybody."

"It absolutely is, and we're doing the best we can in the odd circumstances we now find ourselves."

"Right," she murmured. "And that just opens up the wound about it not being their daughter."

"Exactly, and not being their daughter means that we still have an open cold case."

She pondered that as they walked down almost to the end of the river.

He looked up and asked, "Do you want to pop in and say hi to Nan?"

Mugs, as if hearing and understanding exactly what Mack said, took off toward Rosemoor.

Doreen called for him, "Mugs, get back here. Come on, Mugs. … Get back here."

But he was racing toward Nan's patio. Doreen and Mack came around the corner to find him sitting there, wagging his tail in a crazy way, as he barked outside Nan's patio door. They were just coming up to her place, when the long curtain was pulled to one side, and Nan looked out.

She quickly opened the door. "Goodness, Mugs. What are you doing here?" Then she looked up to see Doreen and Mack coming quickly around the corner. "Did he get away from you?" she asked, chuckling.

"He decided that he should come for a visit," Doreen shared, as she stepped onto the patio.

"That's a smart dog," Nan declared, "and he knows he's well-loved here."

"Oh, he's well-loved at home too," Doreen stated, glaring down at the dog who appeared to have absolutely no compunction about leading them to Nan's.

"We were walking along the creek, and Mack just asked me if we should pop down and say hello, and that's all it took for Mugs to take off."

"You asked and he answered," Nan stated in a complacent tone. "And, of course, he knows where his friends are."

"Sure, he does," Doreen agreed. "It would also be nice if he would listen when called, especially when he's not on a leash."

"*Nah*," Nan argued. "He needs to have a certain amount of his own brilliance on show at all times. Otherwise, how will anybody ever think he's the good detective that he is?"

Doreen rolled her eyes. "It would be nice if he would at least listen."

"We both know that is not happening, is it, buddy?" And she crouched to give him a great big cuddle, just as Goliath jumped over Mugs and landed half in her arms and half on the floor.

Nan gave a bit of a yelp and then burst out laughing. "Oh my, you guys are so good for my soul."

"According to them, you must be feeling as if you need some love and attention today," Mack noted, with a smile.

She looked up at him and nodded. "And I won't say it wasn't a bit of a lonely day or that I wasn't feeling a little bit down, but they certainly did pick up on it."

"Is there any particular issue?" he asked, frowning.

"No, it's just one of those days where you don't feel 100 percent." She stood up, smiled at him, and added, "Thanks for bringing Doreen down."

"I think you owe Mugs a *thank you* for that."

"Ah, but you asked Mugs if he wanted to come."

"So, that's a big yes for visiting you." He smiled as they all stepped inside, and Nan rushed to put on the teakettle.

Doreen added, "We're fine. Don't fuss over us. We just needed to get out for a little bit of fresh air."

"Exactly, winter can get a little bit hard when you're stuck inside all the time," Nan noted, "but, if you can get outside, that's all the better."

"Do you need to get out? Do you feel a little bit penned in yourself?" Doreen asked quickly. "Do you want to go shopping? Do you want to go to the mall or something?"

Nan smiled at her granddaughter. "A day's outing would be lovely. I know that technically speaking we were just out, with that trip to the Rutland park, but this would be even better."

"Sure," Doreen agreed. "We can go to the mall, if you want."

"Do you need anything?" Nan asked.

"No, I don't," Doreen replied.

Beside her, Mack sighed. "She won't say if she does or she doesn't anyway." Mack gave Doreen *the look*. "She's still not sure if she has any money to spend or not." Then he recounted the discussion about her not buying Chinese food.

Nan stared from Mack to Doreen, then back to Mack, her eyes wide and her eyebrows shooting up to her hairline. "Good Lord, child." Then she frowned and asked, "Is that my coat?"

"Yes, it is. I love it." Doreen did a little twirl. "Still wearing it. It's very high-quality."

Nan tilted her head. "That may be, but have you bought yourself anything? Any clothing, anything at all?"

Doreen shrugged. "Not yet, not until I get the money."

At that, Nan just frowned and glanced over at Mack, who nodded at her. "You know you have money, right, dear?"

"I have some money," she pointed out. "But I don't know how much money I have, and I don't know how much money is coming. So, until I'm comfortable knowing that I have enough, I'm not spending it," she declared, with a touch of asperity.

Nan stepped back a bit. "That's fine. I'm not trying to make you spend money. I just need you to be aware that you're okay and that you have money enough for whatever you want."

"Do I though?" she asked, staring at Nan. "Because I'm not so sure about that." And then she proceeded to tell her what she wanted to do with the money.

"If you spend it by the millions, maybe you won't have as much as I thought," Nan conceded. "Yet you also have to live, child, and you've spent all your time since you got here trying to live on nothing."

"That's because I had nothing," she pointed out. "I mean, if it wasn't for you slipping me money here and there, I wouldn't have been able to pay the bills."

"I think you would have been just fine," she muttered, smiling at her granddaughter. "You have been incredibly resourceful. Hasn't she?" She turned and looked at Mack, and he nodded.

"Just with the little bit of gardening money and your grandmother's that I even know about," he replied,

"Doreen's done remarkably well."

Doreen wasn't completely convinced. She shrugged. "I will spend some when I feel I can afford it and not before." Nan frowned at that, but Doreen was adamant. "I won't start spending money until I have a good idea of the total," she declared. "Until then I will be frugal."

Chapter 13

THE NEXT DAY Doreen woke feeling slightly out of sorts and chomping at the bit to get some progress on something—on anything at this point. The trouble was, there wasn't anything to progress on, and that was frustrating too. It shouldn't be this hard to get somewhere, especially when she was dealing with three cases. But the only lead she had was that older couple, and that wasn't exactly a lead at all.

Determined to at least get out and take a fresh look, she bundled up the animals and headed back up to the park. It was a little easier to find this time, and she drove around, trying to see where it started and stopped and the general location of the area it was in. When she finally parked and got out, Mugs gave her a look as if to say it was about time.

He wandered around the park, happy that the place was empty and that he had it all to himself—except for Goliath, who gave him a swipe as the cat rounded on the dog. Then again, the weather wasn't terribly nice, so Doreen wasn't sure that many people wanted to be out in it just yet. Maybe after the sun had a few hours to warm things up a little bit.

Doreen watched Mugs wander around, content, just

snuffling away. Thaddeus remained quiet on her shoulder, snuggling in closer to her to stay warm. Goliath, on the other hand, had taken a perch up on a bench and just stayed there. She walked over, sat down beside the huge Maine coon cat, and began to pet him. "You okay, big guy?"

He looked back at her, but that phrase alone was enough to send Thaddeus crowing from her shoulder, "Big Guy, Big Guy, Big Guy."

"No, we won't visit Big Guy today."

But he wouldn't be stopped. "Big Guy, Big Guy, Big Guy." And, with that, he bounced over to where the grave was and just hopped up and down again. "Big Guy, Big Guy, Big Guy."

Slowly she got up, walked over to him, not sure what he was up to. "You're right. The body here was of a big guy."

Thaddeus continued. "Big Guy, Big Guy, Big Guy."

She frowned in exasperation. "I'm not sure that's helping, Thaddeus."

"You're talking to that bird," declared a woman nearby, her astonishment evident, both on her face and in her tone.

Doreen turned to find an older woman. "Sure," she replied, with a shrug. "Why not? He's my pet, after all."

"I didn't think people kept animals like that. Surely it's not healthy for them."

"Not healthy?" Doreen repeated, turning to look at her. "What do you mean? He's a perfectly happy, normal bird."

"But he's still a bird, and it's not common to keep birds as pets."

Doreen stared at her. "They certainly are common in my world."

The other woman flushed. "I didn't mean any insult by it."

But Doreen wasn't so sure, since such disdain had filled her tone.

"I mean, don't they poop everywhere?" asked the woman. "Imagine cleaning that up all the time."

Doreen just stared at her, willing her to disappear. This woman obviously had never been around animals at all and surely had never had a pet. The park had been nice, friendly, and generally peaceful—until this woman had showed up.

The woman looked around, saw the crime scene tape, and shivered. "Just imagine, a body's been hidden here this whole time," she muttered.

"Kind of scary, isn't it?" Doreen murmured.

"More than scary. I mean, … I've lived here for a very long time, and it never would have occurred to me that anything like this was here. That poor person."

"It was a man," Doreen shared helpfully, "and a tall one at that. He's six-and-a-half-feet-plus-tall or some such thing," she added, with a wave of her hand.

"Oh my, you're right. That is tall."

Doreen didn't say a whole lot and just watched as the other woman frowned, her gaze going uneasily back to Thaddeus and then over to the bench where Goliath sat.

"Is that your cat too?" she asked. "And the bird? The cat doesn't attack the bird?"

Doreen shook her head. "No, he doesn't, and, yes, the bird, the cat, and the dog are mine."

"What dog?" And then she saw Mugs snuffling his way through some underbrush. "Interesting," she muttered, and then she sat down abruptly on the bench with Goliath. "Are you that detective person?"

"I don't know about being a detective person," Doreen clarified, "but I have certainly been involved in solving a bunch of crimes locally."

"I heard the detective lady had all kinds of birds and animals. I just never thought to see you in person. Doreen, isn't it?"

Doreen nodded but could see the confusion on the woman's face, as if she didn't know to be disgruntled or thrilled about it. "Yes, I'm Doreen. I also live in town," Doreen noted. "So it makes sense that we would cross paths at some point."

"Yes, yes, of course. I'm Meghan by the way," she added, with a wave of her hand. "Sorry, I didn't mean to be intrusive." She looked back at the hole in the ground, marked off by police tape, and muttered, "The grave is just upsetting."

"Yes, of course," she murmured. "It's hard to imagine how long he was here."

She looked at her and asked, "Do you know anything about it?"

"No, not a whole lot," Doreen replied. "The police haven't been able to find out very much yet."

"I figured you would be all over it."

"Only so much I can be *all over*. I mean, we're looking for people who have been missing possibly thirty-plus years, without a whole lot of information on them. So not much I can go on, and, of course, there's another missing person too."

"Oh, who's that?" asked Meghan, settling back ever-so-slightly on the bench, keeping a wary gaze on Goliath.

"One body was misidentified," Doreen noted, "but we're close to finding out who that one is."

"Oh goodness," Meghan muttered. "I knew somebody who went missing, but that was a very long time ago. I think they moved on to Alberta."

"Of course, that's always the problem, isn't it?" Doreen said, looking at her. "You think somebody's moved to Alberta, but, in reality, for all you know, they went six feet under." Then she pointed to the grave.

Meghan shuddered. "I really don't think I could handle that. He was a very gentle person, and he might have had … He might have had some issues mentally. I'm pretty sure he did. An accident broke both his legs, and he never did recover. Not sure if he wasn't a bit … slow mentally too. I think that was from the accident as well."

Doreen stared at her. "And who was this?" she asked, holding her breath.

The woman frowned, stared off in the distance. "I think his name was something like Eli, … but it's hard to remember. It was so long ago."

"And how did you know him?" she asked.

"I went to school with him a long time ago, but he was held behind many years because of his disability," she explained. "He spent a lot of years at school. He never did finish, or at least I don't think he finished."

Doreen nodded. "So his broken legs were not his only disability?"

She frowned, shook her head, and sighed. "I'm ashamed to say it, but we thought he was definitely, you know, not quite all there. … A lot of us weren't the kindest to him. Only after I left high school did I realize just how cruel the real world is, and I could see that maybe he hadn't had an easy time of it."

"If the schoolkids were mean to him, I'm sure he didn't have an easy time of it," Doreen noted. "And how did he break both legs?"

"I'm not sure. He didn't talk a whole lot, and we didn't volunteer to be very friendly."

Doreen read between the lines. "Meaning that you and your childhood friends were quite the bullies."

The other woman glared at her, and then her shoulders slumped. "In hindsight, yes, we probably were. We were young and thought we owned the place. We didn't understand what was waiting for us when we grew up."

"You're still alive, so obviously it wasn't too bad for you."

"I married an abusive man," she shared, her gaze darting around. "And I never did have any children. So now I'm facing a lot of *old lady years* in front of me, all alone. I'm not sure that would suggest I did *okay*."

Doreen considered herself *okay*, and she had had an abusive marriage too. Still, she didn't feel like sharing that with Meghan.

Meghan shrugged. "I know nobody cares. I think that's one of the hardest lessons. When you get old, nobody cares. When you're young, and you have family, maybe somebody cares. Then suddenly you're too old for anybody to think about. You're supposed to be an adult and capable of taking care of yourself. When you divorce, people expect you to live your life the way you want to, doing all the things you think you'll enjoy," she muttered, staring around. "Only to find out the things that you thought you enjoyed weren't necessarily anything you enjoyed at all, and you were just doing them because everybody else was. Like getting married. I would have been much better off if I hadn't."

"Are you still married?"

She shook her head. "No, no. ... He took off a long time ago," she muttered. "As much as I was better off, he also didn't leave the paperwork all nice and tidy, so it was quite a few years before I could get that all straightened away."

"Did you ever see him again?"

"No, I sure didn't," she said, followed by a heavy sigh. "I figured he took off with somebody's underage daughter. Of course I hadn't seen a bunch of people from back in that era either." She gave a wave of her hand. "Once I got married, my husband more or less worked at isolating me from everyone," she noted in an odd tone. "It took until he left for things to really ease up for me."

"I'm sorry about that," Doreen replied. "That makes it pretty tough."

"It does make it very tough," Meghan confirmed, looking at her. "And you do what you can, but you don't always get the option of getting away."

Doreen thought about it long after the woman had left. Then Doreen got up and headed toward the other side of the park, where she and Mack had driven the other day, trying to find where the older couple had walked off to. She was trying to figure out in her mind how to broach Meghan and to get a name from her as to who it was she hadn't seen in years. Yet Doreen expected Meghan to be extremely touchy about anybody talking to her. Just as she had been while in the park.

As she came around the corner, Meghan was coming down a different way and seemed startled to see her.

Doreen smiled. "That's funny to see you here. I just left on this side."

"I often keep walking," Meghan admitted. "It's lonely days."

"Winter can be that way," Doreen shared. "Just checking. You don't remember the name of that guy who went missing, *huh*?"

"I told you it was something weird like Eli."

"Right. Well, here's my card, if you come up with his last name …"

"What difference would it make?" Meghan asked, frowning at her. "I mean, it's just one of many people I lost touch with over the years."

"I understand that," Doreen replied. "We don't have any leads, so anything we can come up with would be a help."

"That guy is just like I said, one of many."

"Of course." Doreen forced herself to smile at Meghan and gave her a nod. Doreen kept on walking, after giving Meghan her card. As she walked ahead, she saw the back of an older woman. This was the same older woman she had spoken to the other day, when she'd been at the park with her grouchy husband.

Doreen sped up so that she was close to catching her, and then watched as the other woman headed across the street and back up to the same house that she had walked to before.

Doreen hesitated, but she didn't really have any questions to ask or anything to bother her about. Not sure why the impulse was so strong to go talk to her. Yet, knowing that she didn't have any reason to right now, she slowly turned back. And then found Meghan staring at her from the end of the block.

"It almost looked as if you wanted to talk to her."

"A part of me says I should talk to her, but I really don't have any specific questions to ask."

"If you're trying to find people who have been missing for years and years, that couple could probably help you, as they have been around here since forever."

Doreen nodded. "And yet when I did speak to them not all that long ago, they didn't have anything to offer. They're probably too scared to talk to the police anyway. The old man didn't seem to be all that friendly."

She snorted. "No, he's not very friendly at all. He's kind of like my husband, and I suspect she's found herself in exactly the same situation."

"And what is that?" Doreen asked.

"Left with a controlling husband, and you don't have anything, no family or friends left once they're done with you. And that was me. I've tried hard, but it's been very difficult to get to know people."

"I'm not sure what age category you're looking to become friends with," Doreen began, "but I'm sure quite a few people in town are in the same boat."

"Maybe they are, but that doesn't mean that any of us feel comfortable reaching out," Meghan shared. She looked back at the park and shuddered. "You really are trying to figure out what's going on here, aren't you?"

"I sure am," Doreen declared, "and, yeah, it makes me seem nosy, and some people don't like that."

"Of course not," Meghan agreed. "You really are just ready to pounce with questions."

"I do ask a lot of questions, and again some people don't like it," Doreen acknowledged, with a cheerful smile. "I tend to alienate myself too."

Meghan frowned at her. "Then why do it?"

"Because I'm not particularly worried about how people view me," she explained. "I'm much more concerned about finding justice for all these victims."

Meghan nodded slowly. "In theory I get it, but the cost,

the personal cost to you, is really high."

"That depends," Doreen replied. "There will always be people who see it from that point of view, and then other people see it differently. I think we each need to find our tribe, the people who think about things our way versus other ways. In other words, I hang around people who see that I'm doing a good job and who appreciate what I'm doing, versus people who just think I'm being nosy."

"Well, of course." Meghan laughed. "Everybody wants people to like them."

"I don't even think it's about being liked," Doreen corrected, smiling at Meghan. "That's not really anything I'm particularly bothered about. I'm much more concerned about knowing that these victims and their families find closure. Look at you. You don't know what happened to this Eli person, who you know, and yet he's on your mind every once in a while."

"Sure, but more because I feel so guilty."

Doreen nodded. "And that says more about you than you know. If you think of anything, any specifics about him, just let me know, and I can add it to the growing database I have of missing people." She wasn't lying, and technically it was growing. She didn't say a whole lot about what was growing, but, as she didn't have a ton to go on, she was trying to deal with some definite issues here.

Meghan looked at her and nodded slowly. "You seem to think I know more than I do," she said finally.

"I think everybody knows more than they expect," Doreen replied, shrugging. "It's just one among many facts of life. You don't know what's important, and, because of that, you don't think your answer is important. And I get that, but nobody is expecting you to know everything.

However, if you have even that one little bit that's helpful, it could be the missing piece, and you don't even know it."

"It would be interesting to solve some of this. And the reason I'm curious about what happened to Eli is that he was a nice guy."

"And you just treated him that way because everybody did, is that it?"

"Yeah, and, looking back, I feel terrible about it."

"Did he appear to be upset at the way everybody treated him?"

She frowned, then shook her head. "No, not really. I think, in a way, he was just used to it or even expected it, I don't know," she muttered. "It sounds terrible to even say it that way."

"It might sound terrible, but we also know that people do some pretty rotten things, and you don't necessarily have any idea where they're coming from or why it happened, but it did. So you just go with it."

"Maybe." Meghan didn't seem to be too happy with that explanation.

"If you think of anything else, let me know."

Feeling that had been a very odd conversation, Doreen headed back across the park to the other side where she had parked her car. As she turned, Meghan still stared at her.

Doreen frowned, wondering exactly what was going on here. When Meghan didn't do or say anything else, Doreen waved, and, not waiting for a response, she got her animals into her vehicle and started to drive home. Only as she put her car into Drive and pulled out onto the road did Meghan wave and shout something. Doreen hit the brakes, then frowned and wondered if she was supposed to go see Meghan, who was now headed over to her.

As soon as she got abreast of her, Meghan asked, "He's dead, isn't he?"

Doreen looked at her and sighed. "I don't know. I don't know anything about Eli, but I will try to find out. I would definitely need a little bit more than his first name though. Right now, he is just Eli, and I need more."

Meghan winced. "Eli, but I can't think of the last name. It's been so long. Honestly I'm not sure I ever knew it. He was years ahead of me at Kelowna Secondary school. No clue where he went before then."

"Okay, if you come up with anything else, I'll try to find out more about him, but there could be nothing."

"Right," she muttered, turning to look at the grave. "He was really tall."

And such sadness filled her tone that Doreen asked her again, "What's the reason behind your concern though?"

Meghan hesitated, then nodded. "I know that you're trying to get me to admit something," she began, "but, even at this stage in my life, it will be very hard for me to go against what everybody had us doing back then."

"You mean, generally being mean to people?"

"Yeah, generally being mean to people," she repeated. "I know it was wrong. I mean, I really know it was wrong. I just didn't have any way to get away from what everybody else was doing, so I could be free of it."

Doreen suggested, "Sometimes you just have to be you and don't let anybody else tell you what *you* should look like."

"It's not that easy," Meghan declared, frowning at Doreen. "Back then, some really big people would have been upset."

Doreen stared at her. "What do you mean by that?"

"I mean, there are always bosses, and I was weak. And, if you didn't do what everybody else told you to do, well, you didn't get anywhere."

"And you wanted to get somewhere?" Doreen asked.

"We all wanted to get somewhere," she cried out. "You can't blame me for that."

"I'm not blaming you for anything," Doreen stated, staring at her. "Really, I'm not. You're blaming yourself."

Meghan started to cry. "He was really sweet, and everybody was so ugly to him."

"Would they have treated him ugly enough to have killed him?"

The woman stared at her in shock, then looked back at the grave and shuddered. "I don't know. … I don't know."

And, with that, she turned and bolted in the opposite direction of the park.

Chapter 14

DOREEN WOKE UP the next morning with the name Eli running through her head again. She had done some preliminary research into the name but hadn't come up with anything, either as a missing person or even as a student who went to school here. She sent Nan a quick text, asking if she knew of an Eli in town from way back when who might have been physically or even mentally challenged.

Nan called her back, her tone lively with curiosity. "That's a very broad spectrum you just asked me for."

"I know," Doreen admitted, with a laugh. "I couldn't really make it much clearer."

"You couldn't make it *less* clear," Nan teased, with a laugh. "Now, do you want to explain?"

"All I can tell you is the conversation I had with a woman down at the park, where we found the body."

"Ooh, now that's interesting."

"I don't know how interesting it is, but it seems to me that somebody should have missed this man."

"I'm sure somebody did," Nan declared. "Still doesn't mean that whoever did is still around."

"I know. I know," Doreen muttered, "and, of course, as

the years go by, we lose more and more people who can give us answers."

"Exactly," Nan stated, "so, we have to be on this one fast."

"I'm trying," Doreen replied. "I was down there earlier at the park with Mack, talking to that one older couple. Then yesterday I went back and spoke to this middle-aged lady about it, but the only lead I've gotten so far is the first name Eli."

She didn't mention Meghan's name or how the wife of the older couple seemed to just disappear, as if she was afraid Doreen would want to talk to her—which of course was true. That was just one of the things she was tossing around in her mind. Apparently she was now getting a bad name for interfering in people's lives, and that's not what she wanted. Yet, if they had any answers, Doreen needed to hear them.

"Earth to Doreen," Nan said in exasperation.

"Oh, sorry," she muttered, giving herself a headshake. "I just drifted off there."

"Yeah, I know," Nan stated. "Now, when do you need answers on this Eli person?"

"Yesterday," Doreen replied cheerfully.

"Of course, of course, silly question. Look. I'm just heading to breakfast, so I can bring up the topic while I'm there, see if anyone knows of anyone named Eli who went missing many, many years ago."

"And he would be close to sixty maybe sixty-five now, if he'd lived."

"Right. I guess you could always talk to one of the mental health centers around town." Then Nan disconnected.

"Yes, but ..." What did *mental issues* mean? Did Eli have ADHD, or did he have a split personality? Was he bipolar?

Or was it not a mental illness but a physical disability? Or was it just the perception of being *off*? What did that mean today? The way people viewed disabilities back then compared to today was a completely different issue.

As Doreen made coffee and scrambled a few eggs over a piece of toast, she wondered about all the people out there in the world and how people's perceptions changed over time. Of course, so many people worldwide didn't have the benefit of the mental health clinics and free medical care that happened up here. It all just left her with even more questions, as she went back to her computer and started searching.

When Dr. Elizabeth Harley called her a little later, Doreen smiled into her phone. "I'm really glad to hear from you. I was getting quite bored."

"Ha," Elizabeth said. "So, you're right. We do have a first go-round, where the remains first ID'd as the senator's daughter could be those of Sandy Wayne—the young woman you contacted me about."

"Oh my. Really?"

"Yes." Elizabeth went quiet. "We have contacted the family, looking for current DNA from them. Once we get that, I'll compare the two samples, and I will get it done as fast as I can."

"Right, back to that DNA process."

"Yes, indeed."

"Do you have any idea how many rape kits haven't been processed for DNA, due to budget limitations?"

"I have no idea. I know it's a huge problem in some places, but I don't think it is here."

"Okay, that would make me feel better."

"Why?"

"If I wanted to help in that area, with a donation, I just wondered where the money could best be used."

"I have to admit that's a heck of an idea," Elizabeth replied, her voice rising. "If you do want to do that, I know some people I could put you in touch with. The hospital is also always looking for money, and I'm sure women's shelters and various places could always use a little bit of extra funding."

Doreen added, "The challenge is that there are also animal shelters that need the funding, but I'm trying to look for places and issues that get overlooked, you know? That's what I'm wondering about right now."

"Keep wondering, and I'm sure you'll come around to your passion project," Elizabeth shared. "I've let Mack know about the potential match, but we're waiting for DNA from the family because of the problems the first time around," she added, "so it'll still be a while."

"Okay. Presumably the family is coming back up to visit?"

"I believe they are planning on flying in this evening," Elizabeth shared, "and we'll go from there. It's so sad to think that maybe their missing daughter has already been buried and misidentified, while they've been out looking for her all this time."

"And, if so, we're still missing the senator's daughter," Doreen pointed out.

"I know, and that just aggravates this situation even more. Maybe, while you're bored, you can go find that person too."

"Ha. It wasn't exactly boredom that brought this one into our life, but I hear you."

"I'm glad you've got nothing better to do with your

time," Elizabeth muttered, "but I've got to run." And, with that, she ended the call.

Her strange comment left Doreen staring down at the phone. Mack called a few minutes later.

"Did I call you first or did Elizabeth get there first?" Mack asked.

"Elizabeth got there first," she confirmed, with half a laugh. "Then she suggested that it was a good thing I have all this free time on my hands, suggesting that I should go find the senator's daughter's body too."

At that, Mack snorted. "She really doesn't know what you do, you know?"

"Of course not," Doreen muttered, "and, for a lot of people, I don't do anything."

"I guess that's what they would see, not having all the information to make a proper decision," he replied. "Does that bother you?"

"No, I don't think it bothers me. ... I could let it bother me, but I can't be bothered to let it bother me."

"Okay, that's a good answer," he said. "As long as you keep solving cold cases, I'm not sure any of these comments will get to you anyway."

"Especially if you let me stay busy on these cold cases, but that's a different story."

"Ah, here we go again."

"Not necessarily," she replied, with a chuckle. "I'm just trying to figure out what this Eli may or may not have to do with anything."

There was a moment of silence. "Eli?" Mack asked in an odd tone.

"Yeah, Eli."

"What Eli?"

"What do you mean, what Eli?" she asked, then shook her head. "Oh, I didn't tell you."

"No, apparently you didn't," he stated in exasperation. "Do you want to fill me in now?"

"I just went back to the park. I was feeling really caged in," she began, "and so I went back and just walked around. An older woman approached me, talking about how bad it was that a grave was right there all this time and how sad it was for some to think that their loved one could have been left like that." Doreen took a moment, then took a deep breath.

"Anyway, after chatting a bit, I realized she'd been in the area a very long time, so I asked if she had any ideas of someone she'd lost touch with or who may have gone missing. The only name she could come up with was Eli. It took a bit more conversation, but, as it turns out, this Eli was a very tall man. She had lost touch with him, as everyone did, because he was unloved in the sense that she thought he had some mental problem or disability. He also had several broken bones, leg bones, and they didn't necessarily think that he was all there."

Dead silence came from the other end of the call. "Good God," Mack muttered.

"I know, but I wasn't expecting to come up with somebody who was feeling guilty because of this."

"No, of course not. Look. You're just triggering something here for me. I'll call you back." He quickly ended the call.

Doreen frowned, wishing he had been a little more forthcoming, but that was Mack. So she would just take what she could get and would let him be who he was. Which, honest to God, she was pretty lucky that he was who he was.

Knowing that now she would have to sit here and wait, which would drive her nuts, she turned her attention to the other topic, absolutely delighted to think they may have already found out the remains ID'd as the senator's daughter were really this other young woman, the Sandy Wayne from Solomon's files. Doreen knew it would be a while to get the DNA confirmed, but still, it was something to consider as almost solved. Once again, they had answers, just not solid answers, not matching answers, and not enough of them. Not yet.

She pondered that as she flipped through this morning's local printed newspaper. There was no mention of the body found in the park, not even a mention of any remains being found. Which was a bit of a surprise to her. Of course, there was no mention as of yet of the identity of the woman who had been misidentified as the senator's daughter. It was too early.

Doreen groaned as she realized that everybody else was off doing something, and she was not. Frustrated, she went back to her laptop and started looking for Eli. Any Eli. Getting creative with her search, she then started looking for institutions where somebody named Eli may have resided.

Not finding anything or even what that particular service would be called, she wondered who she could ask. Almost immediately she thought about Nan and the Rosemoor home, wondering if they took in people who had mental disabilities. She quickly picked up the phone, not giving herself a chance to question her impulse and contacted the manager down there. He was, as always, jovial and, in this case, happy to hear from her.

"Hey, Doreen," he greeted her. "What can I help you with?"

She began, "Do you take inmates—residents, I mean," she quickly corrected herself, "who have mental disabilities?"

"It depends on what the disability is and how much care they require," he replied, "and don't forget that everything is on a tiered system here. So, if they need a certain level of care, and it's minimal, we could probably take them, depending on what the problem is."

"Can you explain the process?"

"If they required a higher level of care, not only would the cost be much higher but there also could be a need for something that we can't provide here at Rosemoor," he explained. "For example, if you had somebody who required more physical lifting—say, help to get to the bathroom, to the dining room, in and out of bed, those things—we would need to elevate them to a facility with a higher level of care, where they had beds with lifts and other special equipment to help people get in and out for bathing and whatnot. Now, in the case of mental disability or mental illness, it's never quite so clear-cut. They have to get along with people, and it has to be something that we can manage here." He sounded almost worried. "Doreen, are you trying to find a place for someone?"

"No, no, no," she said. "Sorry, I didn't mean to give that impression. To be honest, I'm working on a case."

"Oh my," he replied in amazement. "I don't know how I can help with that, other than—"

"No, you've provided exactly what I needed," she stated. "Is there a facility here in town that handles the more difficult situations?"

"Oh yes, of course." He mentioned two specialized manors in town. "One is run by the government, and the other is private."

"Right, so the private one is likely to be very expensive."

"Yes. And, when we say, *expensive*, I mean very expensive."

"Right," she muttered. "It always ends up that way, doesn't it?"

"Looking after someone twenty-four hours a day," he noted, clicking his tongue, "is inherently expensive, and there's really no way to make it easier on anybody. So a lot of people have to come together to make that doable."

"I'm not criticizing you," she pointed out. "I'm just really trying to figure out how this could be."

"How what could be?"

"What it would take for somebody to live in such a home, versus one of those more specialized homes."

"It's ultimately all about capacity," he added. "The homes go through a series of tests, getting assessments done as to who we bring in as residents. We need to determine if each individual will be in a regular long-term assisted living situation, such as here at Rosemoor, or if they need to go into a skilled nursing environment or something more specialized, like memory care or other mental health scenarios," he described. "That's just one of the facts of life. At this stage, the patients need the assessment in order for us to follow up on what their needs are, where they are better placed."

"Okay, that's good to know," Doreen said. "I'll reach out to these two manors and see if they have the information I need."

"Sure enough, glad to help." He added, "I did hear a few murmurs about you possibly wanting to have the wedding here. I feel bad saying this, but I'm not sure that is something I can manage."

"Oh no, that was the Rosemoor clan trying to create that opportunity," she corrected. "Believe me that I would totally understand if you told me that it wasn't possible."

"I do understand that you would want to have your grandmother and a lot of other people here with you on that special day, but I'm not sure how we could manage that."

"That's just one of the reasons I haven't worked too quickly to resolve these wedding issues. It'll take some time to figure out what'll work nicely for everyone," she added.

"Oh good. I'm so glad you came to that awareness on your own. We all want you to have an absolutely wonderful day, but I'm just not sure that everybody can be there for it."

"I was wondering if maybe one of the answers was not a duplicate wedding but potentially something like that," she suggested. "Perhaps a small reception just for everybody at Rosemoor. I was also considering doing the whole thing down at Central Park. However, by the time people started talking about the list of people who want to come, ... it sounded as if I won't have any venue big enough."

"You know a park wedding would be absolutely smashing," he cried out. Then he asked, "Can you do that?"

"I have no idea," she muttered. "And that puts me right back into that whole realm of not knowing what is possible."

He chuckled. "The good news is, you have time."

"Yes, I'm very appreciative of that."

"Let us know if we can help in some way," he said, "and we could certainly look at having a small reception for the residents here, just so that everybody feels included. Of course, depending on where you end up having the wedding ceremony, and how many people here at Rosemoor are interested and able to attend, we could also organize a small bus to bring them down. Yet some residents would require a little more care down at the park."

"I know, and they can get into so much trouble," she muttered.

He burst out laughing. "That is very true, but I have to admit that, since you came onboard, they've been so lively and far happier. This place positively hums, and, for that, we are grateful. There's nothing we could possibly have done ourselves to get that kind of joyous atmosphere here. That is literally all down to you. So we are very grateful, and, if we can do anything to help, please just let us know." And, on that note, he rang off.

His words left her smiling with joy in her heart to think that she was contributing in a positive way to that group of seniors. And it wasn't just about Nan. It was the whole Sherlock club and beyond.

She'd already forgotten what they called themselves, but it just made her smile to realize how close-knit everybody had become. If there had been problems before, they had certainly gone out the window, as everybody wanted to be involved and worked hard to be included in every one of her cases now. It made them smile too, and that was worth every bit of the trouble involved.

Chapter 15

DOREEN MADE PHONE calls to both of the homes that the manager of Rosemoor had commented on. Neither had any current residents by the name of Eli. She frowned, knowing that was good news because, if that was Eli in the grave at the park, then he wouldn't be in a home. She wasn't even sure why she had made that call, since it seemed a little foolish, but she couldn't help herself from checking just to see.

When she got a phone call a little bit later, she answered it right away, recognizing it as being from one of the homes.

"Hi," said an older woman. "I heard that you phoned the home about Eli."

"Yes. I just wondered if an Eli was currently at the home."

"There had been, yes," she shared.

Doreen thought the woman's voice was quite creaky, as if beyond old, and yet that was a judgment Doreen couldn't really make with any accuracy. She waited for the other woman to speak, but there was silence. Doreen asked, "And can you tell me anything about him? When did he leave the home? And why? And may I get your name too, if you don't

"

mind my asking?"

"I'm Margaret Gibbons. And we're not sure," she said. "It was a very long time ago."

"I know," Doreen replied, yet feeling something go *click* inside. "Why are you asking about him?"

"Because I'm concerned about his whereabouts."

"We all are, as so many years have passed."

Margaret added, "I'm pretty sure his whereabouts are a nonissue at this point."

"When you say that, what do you mean?" Doreen asked.

"Just that the chances of him having survived are not great."

"Was he mentally incapacitated?" Doreen asked.

"He had a brain tumor that they had operated on when he was younger, and there was some damage that he never fully recovered from," Margaret shared. "He was a lovely person but was given to fits every once in a while. So, his life was limited in the sense that he lived here with us for a long time."

"And you worked at the same home?"

"I used to work at the home many years ago, a place I always called home. I was there what seemed like every day, even the weekends, and I grew very close to the residents."

"And to somebody named Eli?" Doreen asked.

"Yes, very much so. He was a very gentle soul, except for when he was having his turns. Even then it was generally okay, except for if he got off his medications or they needed to be adjusted. Then we would have a period of ups and downs, but eventually he would be fine again."

"What happened to him? Why did he leave the home?"

"I thought his family pulled him out," she replied. "We never knew quite what the story was, but I believe they told us officially that they would be moving to the coast and needed to place him somewhere down there."

"Yet, was he released to the family?"

"I didn't see that myself. There was a time period when the government stopped funding a lot of these institutions, and we did get caught up in that for the longest time. It took the company quite a bit to get the funding that they needed to carry on with the manor. So, for that time period, our management was happy enough for anyone to leave just because we couldn't afford to keep everyone. Still, it was sad to lose Eli because he had been such an institution in and of himself."

"How long was he there?"

"I couldn't say exactly, but probably maybe ten years, even fifteen years. He ended up in a home soon after high school."

"Can you explain that, how he went from a public school to this specialized home?" Doreen asked.

"He was set to graduate with a remedial diploma, something else that they did at the time. Meaning that he had completed his schooling and could go out into the public on his own and work, but the remedial designation also told prospective employers that there were some challenges," she explained. "Still, he was really happy, though his medical problems had been rough. He'd had the brain tumor and the surgery, and there were still quite a few issues which remained from the tumor. Yet the doctor had suggested that Eli would heal and that it would all take time and that, with proper support and care, he could potentially do very well."

"But?"

"But he never really seemed to get the proper time or care, and he never really did show improvement," she shared.

"And I don't know that anybody was to blame for that. All I'm saying is that it was a very difficult time for everyone."

"Of course," Doreen agreed. "I'm not sure anything is worse than knowing that someone you love and care for will struggle like that."

"Exactly, and his mother had to work. I think she ended up passing on in an accident—or cancer. I don't recall. The mother and the grandmother were Eli's main points of care."

"So, who would move him down south then?"

"I believe it was his father. Again you would have to talk to them to confirm."

"Right. Can you give me the rest of the family's names?"

"Oh dear," Margaret muttered. "That's a little harder, just because I don't quite have the same memory anymore."

"Understood," Doreen noted. "If I could get the last name that would be great. However, if I could even get a first name, the father's or the grandmother's or mother's first names, anything like that, I could carry on with my research."

"*Hmm*, I think the mother's name was Mary, and I think … I don't remember the father."

"And the grandmother?"

"I want to say Glenda, but I can't be sure."

"Do you happen to know anybody's surname?"

"Oh dear. The thing is, we got so very close, but surnames were never really part of it."

"Right. When I spoke with the manor, they said they didn't have anybody there right now named Eli."

"No, they don't, not now. Eli hasn't been there for a very long time," Margaret noted. "It is one of the challenges, you know, once they up and move. It's not as if we could keep their records forever. Plus, by the time everything was digitized, most of the old physical files were lost anyway."

Doreen wasn't exactly sure how medical records got lost, but she presumed it was something that could happen. "I'm sorry for everything that the family went through. That had to be harsh."

"He was the only boy, but I think that maybe he wasn't the only child," Margaret shared. "I'm sorry. I just don't remember."

"That's fine," Doreen replied, not wanting Margaret to get so frustrated that she would end the call. "What about Mary and Glenda? What can you tell me about them? Were they locals?"

"Oh, yes, long-term locals. Everybody felt so sorry for Mary. I mean, she'd had quite the time with her son. Then, of course, he was never quite right afterward, which impacted everybody even that much more."

"Of course," Doreen agreed, "it's always hard when people need help but can't get it."

"And Mary didn't have much money, so Eli was a charity case. You would like to think that the government had things in place to provide stable care for him, but it never really was that way. So this element of uncertainty and struggle always remained. There was a time when mental health had the appropriate care, but, in Eli's case, because it was brought on by the surgery and the brain tumor, it didn't quite fit the mental health arena as being something they could just automatically pay for. Mary did get quite a bit of help for a while though."

"So you mentioned the father moved Eli down to the coast."

"Yes, that's what I recall."

"And you don't know where on the coast or what facility

he might have moved to?"

"No, not at all," she said. "The father was very caring, very loving, any time we saw him, but he didn't come all that often."

"I'm sure it was hard on him to see his son in that condition."

"I'm sure it was," Margaret agreed, her voice getting stronger. "That sure didn't stop his mother from coming."

"No, but there is nothing quite like a mother's love," Doreen pointed out.

"You're right there." Margaret's voice seemed to be weaker, as if all the stuffing had been sucked out of her.

"I appreciate the phone call and your information," Doreen said, "and I will try hard to track down somebody in the family, although a surname would certainly help. Did Mary or Glenda run a business? Did they work? Do you know what they did for money?"

"Mary was a cleaning lady in town, but I don't think that company even exists, not past her anyway," Margaret shared, "as she was one of the main forces in it. Just a couple of them worked together, and I know that the other woman she worked with has also passed on."

"What about Glenda?"

"*Hmm*, I'm not sure Glenda ever worked much. ... She was much more the stay-at-home mother and then had various jobs, depending on her home life as a grandmother. At least that's as much as I can remember."

"Of course, and, if she could do that, that's great."

"Exactly, I never could do that myself," Margaret stated, with a laugh. "Paychecks were always needed, and, if one of us could bring home a paycheck, ... then that's what we did."

"How long did you work?"

She replied, "I lost count, though it seemed like forever. I worked right through retirement and then past, thinking we would finally take some time for ourselves, but money was still tight. Then my husband came down with cancer, and that pretty well finished us. He was gone within three months," she recalled, her voice catching. "And, soon enough, I will be gone as well. I'm grateful because I want nothing more than to join him and the rest of my family," she murmured.

"Did you ever have any kids?"

There was a sigh on the other end. "Yes, I did, but unfortunately I lost my daughter and her husband in a car accident."

"Oh my, I'm so sorry."

"I've had a lot of loss in my life. At some point, you just don't want to be the only one left," she explained, "but that's where I'm at."

"Can you think about what the father might have done for a job? Or, if you could come up with a surname, that would help, or somebody who might know of a surname. Did they have any other friends? Anybody else they were close to?"

"It was just the two women in the family as far as I remember," she said. "But my memories get old and fuzzy, and it's hard to keep things clear."

"You've done wonderfully though," Doreen replied, "and it is very much appreciated."

Margaret muttered, "I hope that Eli had a good long life and that he was happy."

"I also heard something about broken legs?"

"Yes, he was in an accident, and the broken legs never

really healed properly. He ended up in a wheelchair fairly quickly, but it was while they were trying to figure out why the legs weren't healing that they discovered the brain tumor," she explained. "So, in a way it was a blessing but, in another way, maybe not."

"Ah, do you know how old he was?"

"Oh goodness no. Yet he would be a senior I think. I highly doubt he's even alive." Her voice dropped for a moment, and then she suddenly seemed energized with curiosity. "I have to wonder why on earth you would be even asking about him. Hardly anybody even knew him."

"I was looking for people who had gone missing in town. In particular, various extremely tall men."

"Eli would have been tall. That's for sure. It's one of the reasons why his legs never quite healed. There was already a weakness, maybe the pituitary or pineal gland, I don't know. I'm sorry. It really was a long time ago."

"I understand. ... Have you heard about the discovery made at the park here?"

"I heard something, but I'm not really sure what it means."

"They found the body of a very tall man in a grave," Doreen shared.

Margaret gave a harsh gasp and then spoke in a shocked whisper, "No, please ... no."

"I'm so sorry," Doreen said, "but that's one of the reasons that I'm trying to find Eli, to see if he is okay, whether he carried on to live a nice long, happy life. I had heard that he was very tall, so—"

"Yes, yes," she confirmed, pain evident in her tone. "He was very tall."

"And obviously we want him to have had as good a life

as he could have."

"Obviously," Margaret agreed, "but you're making it sound as if he didn't."

"I can't make it sound any way other than what it is," Doreen clarified, "which, at the moment, is completely inconclusive. We don't know anything yet."

"Right, so it may not be him."

"Exactly, and I'm not suggesting that it is him. I was literally just trying to find out if people happen to know other tall men or anybody else who went missing or who people lost track of."

"The people I dealt with were all from the home," she noted. "I worked there all my life."

"I presume somebody from the home contacted you about me asking about Eli then."

"Yes. My niece works there."

"Ah, well, I'm glad she did because it's been wonderful to connect with you."

"I hope you're wrong about Eli," Margaret said, her voice deepening.

"I don't know anything at this moment, so keep that in mind. All I know is that they found a body."

"It would be terrible to think that it could be him," she whispered. "He was a very lovely person."

"And we don't know that it was him or that anything bad happened to him," Doreen repeated.

"That's true too. But why bury him out there?"

"I'm not sure everybody had access to proper burials back then."

Margaret went silent for a moment, and then she added, "They did not. You are right about that, and his family was incredibly poor. So these things happened. But, if it had been a death that everybody knew about, people would have come together to confirm Eli was buried. He was well-loved, though not always the easiest to work with. He certainly wasn't always perfect, but none of us are," Margaret shared. "Still, he was a good man who never really had a chance to be any better because of all the challenges that he had. Once the physical challenges came about, the other challenges increased as well. After the brain tumor, he was never quite the same."

"I'm so sorry for him," Doreen whispered, and she meant it. "He sounds as if he would have been a lovely person to know."

"Oh, he was absolutely wonderful," Margaret stated. "If I'd had a son, I would have been more than honored if it had been Eli. But I was never blessed with a boy. I think those in the home just became mine by surrogate," she conceded, with a chuckle. "And thankfully for me they filled a deep emptiness in my heart that I couldn't have filled any other way."

"And that's what we have to hang on to," Doreen pointed out. "Life happens for reasons we sometimes can't understand."

"I always figured it was God's will, and that made it a whole lot easier to deal with," she admitted. "But, if you tell me that it's Eli out there, I sure hope you find out that he died of natural causes and that his family was just too broke and too ashamed of being so broke to bury him properly."

"I will try to give you an update, if and when we ever solve it," Doreen stated. "And, if you do come up with any more tidbits of information, or anybody else who might help, either pass on my phone number or give me a call back."

Chapter 16

AFTER SPEAKING WITH Margaret and letting her go—with at least her contact information secured—Doreen decided to head down to Nan's and see if anybody there knew anything about Margaret, and potentially the mother and the grandmother of Eli. As she walked toward Rosemoor, Nan called her. Doreen froze in her steps. "Problems?"

"No, I was just going to invite you down for tea."

"That's timely," she replied, "because the animals and I are only a few minutes away. We're already on our way to see you."

Nan laughed. "That's perfect timing, since I already put on the teakettle. I'm glad to know we're still in sync."

Doreen ended the call and headed the last little bit to her grandmother's place. She entered from the patio door and smiled as she watched a group of residents all collect in Nan's living room. They made room for her, and she sat down in her designated chair. Her animals wandered around and greeted everybody, hoping for food or a hug. Doreen shook her head. She thought Mugs sometimes just wanted to come so he could get more cuddles.

Doreen cleared her throat and began. "Does anybody know of a Glenda or a Mary, who would have been grandmother or mother respectively to a man named Eli? Mary worked as a cleaner, and Glenda didn't work full-time at anything, as far as we know. There would have been a father too, though I don't have a name or an occupation. Eli apparently had an accident and broke his legs. Then during a subsequent investigation into why he wasn't healing well, among other things such as endocrine problems, they also discovered a brain tumor. He had surgery for the brain tumor, but he never fully recovered. He spent the bulk of his life in a wheelchair, with various issues, physical and mental. This all started when he was young. At well over six feet, he was also very tall for that era."

When they all just looked at her, she nodded. "I'm just hoping to trigger something that could lead to something more. I've got no last names, just given names. I did just speak with Margaret, who worked over at the home where Eli was for a time."

"Margaret Gibbons?" Maisie asked.

Doreen looked down at her notes and then nodded. "Yes, that's her last name."

"Oh, interesting," Maisie noted. "She was always very involved with special needs patients."

"Yes, that's what I understand. She had a daughter who she lost in a car accident, and her husband has since passed on. When she heard I was asking questions about Eli, she reached out. Now, she was told that Eli was moved to the coast. I guess there was some time period where the government stopped funding for a lot of the mental health facilities, and so his father supposedly took Eli down to the coast."

"So, you're wondering if he's actually down there?" Nan

asked.

"I'm wondering if anybody in his family is still alive. That would be our best chance of getting more information on Eli, plus confirming that he did go to the coast."

"You're not thinking that's him in the grave at the park, are you?" Richie asked, staring at her.

"I have absolutely no facts to confirm that's him in the grave," Doreen clarified. "Yet I have no reason to *not* consider it either."

Richie harrumphed and sat back, staring at her. "Sounds like lots of guesswork to me. Mack won't like that."

She smiled at him. "You are absolutely correct. He won't like that, which is why I'm working to find more people who might know about this Eli—or anybody else they've lost track of who was extremely tall. So far, I keep getting blank looks."

Richie snorted. "Losing track of all kinds of people over the years is quite common, but there just aren't that many people who are extremely tall, especially back then," Richie pointed out. "I'm considered tall, but you're saying he was a good couple inches taller than me?"

"Yes," Doreen confirmed. "And, back then, I understand people were even shorter."

"Of course." Richie nodded. "Seems every generation since is getting taller."

She nodded and didn't get any further into that discussion. "So, the question is, does anybody know of Eli, Mary, Glenda?"

Immediately heads started to shake. Yet Maisie had a frown on her face.

"Maisie, what about you?" Doreen asked.

"I'm not sure," she replied.

At that, Nan just rolled her eyes. "How can you *not* be sure, Mace?"

"Because, back then, an awful lot of people were involved in a lot of these mental health cases," she shared. "I was a nurse, you know?" Doreen looked at her in surprise, and Maisie nodded. "But I wasn't dealing with the mental health cases," she added, "so I don't remember Eli. I don't remember anybody with that description. Now obviously we had many tall people come through the hospital, but it's not something that I would have thought of as being different or even unusual."

"No, of course not," Doreen noted. "The thing is, we also can't be sure that many people even noticed how tall Eli was. If he was in a wheelchair, which he was for a large part of his life, then I'm not sure his height would have even been seen. It depends on if he was long and tall in the torso or if he was all legs."

Nan frowned at her and then nodded. "That's a good point because, if you're sitting in a wheelchair, everybody may not even necessarily take that into consideration."

"Exactly," Doreen agreed. "The thing is, the remains found in the Rutland park are of a very tall male, with broken legs," she shared, looking from one resident to the other. "And that, at least, matches Eli's description."

Richie stared at her. "Good Lord, if you've already got that information and it matches this Eli ..."

"Yes, but you know that Mack will still want more."

"Oh, he'll definitely want more," Richie confirmed, "but it's quite surprising that you've found this much so quickly."

She laughed. "And I can see that, for you, it's a surprise, but I would like to think it's less of a surprise for Mack."

Richie just shook his head. "Hard to say. You know as

well as I do that he always wants more proof."

"He does, and I'm more than happy to give it to him if we can get it," she stated. "However, right now, things are a little scarce in that department."

"They are, indeed," he muttered. "They are, indeed. … I can't think of but a couple people in all the years I've been here that was as tall as me—or taller. Nobody ever laughed or joked or made a comment about it."

She stared at him. "Which is interesting, since you are definitely tall but not necessarily the tallest."

"No," he replied, shaking his head, "absolutely not. And you're right. As tall goes, there are certainly men who are a lot taller than me."

"And yet you haven't seen very many."

"No, I sure haven't," he agreed, with a nod. "Nowadays I do see more. I mean, there was a nurse practitioner in acute care, an ACNP, who I swear was seven feet tall. He was here for a little while, and that wasn't all that long ago. I think he ended up transferring down to the coast."

"A seven-foot-tall man would be something," Maisie noted, staring at Richie.

"It was something to see," he admitted. "Yet he appeared to be well-liked and didn't appear to have very many problems."

"That's good to hear," Doreen added. "We would like to think he would have been well received here."

Richie shrugged. "I don't know. When you're different, it doesn't matter if you're tall or chunky or something in-between. That always seems to be a challenge for some people."

"Were you ever given much of a problem over your height?" Nan asked him curiously.

He shook his head. "No, because I'm not hugely out of the norm. Yet, if this Eli as a kid was six foot—or taller than six foot—that may have caused him some issues. However, if he was in a wheelchair, that would have minimized the emphasis on his height."

"But, if he sat up straight, it might be something that most people would recognize," Doreen pointed out.

He nodded. "All I can say is, it still seems as if the information is on the slim side."

"Absolutely it is," she stated, with a smile. "Still working on it. A work in progress, and as you know, that's the goal here."

He smiled. "The fact that you've even found somebody who could fit the description from about thirtyish years ago is pretty amazing."

"But it could all be for naught," she pointed out. "As soon as we get somewhere, we have to get information that validates the rest of it, and that makes it all that much harder."

He just nodded and didn't say anything.

But Doreen returned to Maisie. "Maisie, is something bothering you?"

When Nan went to make another joke about it, Doreen shot her grandmother a look.

Nan shut up, then glared at her. "You're taking all the fun out of life."

Doreen rolled her eyes. "That's hardly *fun* if it hinders us from getting the information we need."

"*Right*," she muttered.

"Maisie," Doreen called out. When Maisie turned to her, Doreen said, "Now spit it out. What is it you're thinking?"

"I thought I remembered something about him." She stopped and shook her head. "I'm sorry. It's hard for me to grab that information just now."

And she looked so upset that Doreen immediately said, "It's all right, Maisie. You have time. Even if you can't think of it right now, don't worry. It will probably come to you later, when you're not trying so hard."

"Oh, thank you," she whispered. "I get so frustrated."

"When you do get frustrated," Doreen pointed out, "it's even harder to get the information you need."

"I know, and it's not that I don't want to help. I really do."

"And I appreciate that," Doreen stated. "Let's just confirm we get the right information at the right time. So anything that anybody can come up with, I need to hear about it. If you find out something else or remember something later, just let me know. But, please, we don't want to stress any of you out."

On that note, she looked down at her animals and asked, "What do you think, guys? Shall we head back?"

Mugs immediately jumped up and headed to the door, making everybody laugh.

She added, "He's always happy to go for a walk." At that, Goliath strolled ahead of him, swiping at Mugs as he walked past.

That sent the crowd into even more laughter.

"The fact that they get along at all," Richie pointed out, "is purely amazing."

She smiled at him. "They really do care about each other," she shared, "even if this *swatting* is so very typical of them."

"Typical of any animal," Richie noted, with half a smile.

"Absolutely normal behavior with siblings."

"That's it. *Siblings*," Maisie cried out. "There was a sibling."

"A sibling? Whose sibling?" Nan asked in exasperation.

Maisie turned to Doreen. "That boy, … Eli. He had a sibling."

"Eli had a sibling? Margaret thought there was possibly a sister or two but didn't remember the details."

Maisie declared, "I'm pretty sure he did."

Richie nodded. "She may very well be right. And just because he had one doesn't mean they came to visit," Richie said, looking over at Maisie. "A lot of families might try to keep something like that a secret, separate from the rest of the family."

"Yeah," Nan interjected, glaring around the room. "There was a time when they believed mental health issues were contagious. Just imagine if poor Eli's already been separated from his family, after going through an accident, brain surgery, sitting in a wheelchair for the rest of his life?"

"So, you're thinking he had a sibling?" Doreen repeated, facing Maisie.

Maisie nodded. "Yes, I think he had a sibling, and there was some concern that the sibling might also have a brain tumor."

"Now that makes sense," Nan replied, facing her granddaughter. "Can you imagine if you already had one child with such a terrible problem, then to find out the second one had the same thing?" Nan shook her head.

"That's an interesting thought," Doreen said, nodding in agreement. "If I could possibly get a last name for this Eli, it would help a lot. But nobody seems to remember."

"We'll put our heads together," Nan suggested, "and

we'll see what we can come up with."

"Good enough," Doreen replied. She walked to the door with her critters and told them, "Now say goodbye."

At that, Thaddeus, waking up from his nap in the fall of her hair, poked his head out and cried out, "Goodbye, goodbye, goodbye."

At that, everybody howled with laughter all over again.

Nan just looked at the African grey parrot and asked, "Thaddeus, where the heck have you been this whole time?"

He yawned. "Thaddeus is tired."

Nan stared at him, then walked up, petted him, and replied, "Not so tired that you aren't still learning new words."

He snuggled against Nan's fingers, but Doreen stated, "Really bad timing though, bud, because we're leaving."

He glared at her, looked back at Nan, and added, "Thaddeus loves Nan."

"Thaddeus, I love you too," Nan declared, with a bright smile. "Now you look after Doreen."

He glared at Doreen and then snuffled in against her shoulder, tucking his head up close, and whispered, "Thaddeus loves Doreen."

"He does seem to be awfully tired today," Nan noted, frowning at Doreen worriedly.

"I think he's fine," Doreen offered. "Every now and then he has days where he just wants to lie around the house."

"Yeah, well, we all have those days," Maisie admitted, with a bright smile.

And, with that, Doreen and her animals headed off.

Chapter 17

THE NEXT DAY Doreen woke up and headed downstairs, her animals at her heels. Her phone started ringing before the coffee had even finished dripping. She groaned at the thought, until she looked down at the screen and read her Caller ID. "Hi, Elizabeth."

"You were right," she stated, without preamble.

"Right about what?"

"The DNA is a match."

It took her a minute to figure out which DNA they were talking about. "Sandy Wayne? Now that is absolutely wonderful news," she cried out in joy. "That's one family who's getting an answer, as much as it's not what they wanted to hear, but at least now they know."

"Exactly, and sometimes that's all we have to give," the coroner noted. "They've been notified of the results, so that is huge for them. Now," Elizabeth added, with a sigh, "what have you found out for the second body?"

Doreen laughed at that. "Am I supposed to have found out something on the second one?"

"I was pretty sure you were working on it."

"I am working on it," she confirmed, "but I don't necessarily have anything very clear-cut yet. However, I am pretty sure that we're looking at the potential remains of one Eli, no last name yet, who was in a bad accident, broke his legs that didn't heal properly, and, during the investigations into that, they ended up finding a brain tumor."

A moment of silence followed on the other end, then a snort. "Oh my," Elizabeth muttered.

"Yes, and I'm still trying to track down his last name. He was a resident at"—she rustled her papers—"at Sky Manor."

"Oh, that's interesting," Elizabeth replied. "I forgot about that place."

Doreen continued. "During a period when apparently the government funding was cut off or reduced, some of these homes were scrambling and suggesting to some families that maybe they needed to take their family members elsewhere because they couldn't afford to look after them anymore. The father supposedly took Eli out, and that's all anybody heard from him. Per the one woman I talked to, she was under the impression that Eli and his father had left for the coast, which would make sense, particularly if Sky Manor didn't have any funding here."

"Yet it's doubtful there would have been funding down there either. The government would have made cuts across the board," Elizabeth pointed out. "Apparently things were pretty rough during that time period, and a lot of patients were literally just put out on the streets. Thankfully that has all turned around now, at least to my knowledge."

"And, if that happened, it would be a little more understandable as to why we're struggling to get any information on Eli."

"It sounds as if you've already got quite a bit of information," Elizabeth said. "I don't know how you do it."

"In this particular cold case I'm sure it's luck," she conceded, with a laugh. "I was literally just talking to people about somebody who was extremely tall and who went missing around thirty years ago. You don't happen to have a possible date of death or a final height on him, do you?"

"So far, the date of death could have been thirty years ago. I'm still working on that, trying to refine it further. However, I would put him at least at six-six, and possibly even more, like six-seven. However, I don't have a proper leg length to go by. His torso was also extremely long, so he could have been even taller than that, but his leg bones never grew properly."

Doreen agreed. "That was apparently one of his issues, and they found an endocrine disorder, involving the pituitary gland or something. Don't quote me on that. Anyway, the accident caused the trouble with his legs, but they didn't heal correctly, so they started finding all these other issues, and he spent most of his time in a wheelchair."

"Poor Eli, and this all started when he was young," Elizabeth added, compassion filling her tone. "That is definitely not an easy life."

"And that aligns with the story from another woman, talking about someone who I presume is the same Eli."

"So, it seems several people did know about Eli."

"I think the fact that he was extremely tall and that he may have had some mental disability is helping to trigger memories."

"That would do it," Elizabeth said, with a groan. "Even if we don't want to remember that stuff, it is what often identifies a person. Often people like Eli can't get rid of that identity either. It winds up being how people label you."

"In this case, it appears that something did trigger somebody who used to work at the home, who vaguely remembers Eli leaving because his father apparently pulled him out. However, she didn't have any more information than that."

"And if there were all these massive budget cuts and if many of the mental hospitals were closing across the provinces, no way to know where Eli could have gone from there."

"Exactly," Doreen muttered. "So, it's not that the trail has gone cold, but it's definitely cooling."

"Yes, I would say so. On the other hand, if it's Eli, he may not have gotten very far at all."

"So, in that case, we would need DNA to test him against."

"True."

Doreen sighed. "So far, I haven't found any family. There might be a mother and a grandmother, for which I have just first names, Mary, who passed from cancer, and Glenda."

"Is that it?"

"Yes, and I know it's the bare minimum," Doreen conceded. "I don't have a surname yet."

Elizabeth groaned. "People always just seem to remember parts and pieces, and it's very frustrating."

"Yes, it is. However, I've got all of Rosemoor on it, and some people there have very long memories. I'll go over to Sky Manor and see if I can pull any archival records. I think I'll start at the library though."

"Oh, that's a great idea. We do need a name, at least more of a name than this in order to search our database records."

"I guess you can't search by first name, can you?"

"We could, but it'll come up with hundreds if not thousands of matches."

"And what about if you add a filter for some mental issues or for a wheelchair or for broken legs?"

"I'll take a look," Elizabeth replied, but she didn't sound very positive. "I just know that, as a general rule, we need a whole lot more. Sometimes even the last name isn't enough. It can give us a starting point, but that's about it."

"Of course," Doreen said.

After hanging up, Doreen quickly checked on the coffee, as her mind ran through the issues. She needed to go to the library, maybe later to Sky Manor. As she looked down at the animals, she apologized. "Sorry, guys. I can't take you to the library with me, but I won't be very long, I think." Then she checked the time, deciding to take the coffee in a travel mug and hoping her drink would be allowed inside the library. She quickly found out that was a hard no, so she groaned as she returned the cup to her car and headed back inside again.

The librarian glared at her. "For somebody who's been here as often as you have, you should really know that rule by now."

"I just forgot," Doreen said. "I missed my coffee at home, and it never occurred to me *not* to bring it. I just thought I would have it while I was here doing research."

The other woman sniffed, as if she didn't believe her and then proceeded to ignore her.

That suited Doreen. The last thing she wanted was anybody else looking over her shoulder while she tried to sort out some of this information.

She started searching for any name with Eli in it and then with variations of spellings that she had to search Google in order to find in the first place. Forty minutes later, she gave that up and searched into Sky Manor and the history of it. There was a little bit of information on the specialized home but not a whole lot. And then she went into articles about cutting the funding for mental hospitals. That led to a deluge of other articles as well, but nothing mentioned Eli personally, and why would they? As she kept digging and digging, she looked over to see a lavender-haired lady sitting off to the side, mumbling to herself.

Doreen glanced at her several more times, and the woman looked up and smiled back, but they each just went back to whatever they were doing. The lady looked to be researching some pattern. At least the book was on medieval patterns.

When Doreen finally sat back, frustrated, and groaned, the other lady smiled and finally spoke. "Now that doesn't sound very positive."

"You know how it is. You try hard to find the information, but it'll be locked up in somebody's head. Since that person isn't somebody I know, I can't just turn around and unlock it."

Her eyes widened. "Now that sounds very mysterious."

"No, not at all," Doreen noted, with a laugh. "I'm just trying to find some information about a patient who had been at Sky Manor many, many years ago."

Her eyes widened. "Now that's even more interesting," she replied, "because my mother used to work there."

Doreen asked her, "Is your mother still alive?"

The other lady shook her head. "No, sorry. She's been gone quite a few years."

"Ah, that's the problem with trying to find out anything back from those days, since most of the people are gone already."

"Depending on how far gone you're talking," she added, rolling her eyes, "I might be able to help."

"I'm trying to locate a young man, a young man at the time, back maybe thirty to forty years ago, I mean," she clarified, with a wave of her hand. "He would be, I don't know, maybe sixtyish now. He was in a wheelchair because he'd had badly broken legs that hadn't healed properly. As they investigated that, among other things, they discovered he had a brain tumor."

"Oh, you're talking about Eli," she exclaimed in astonishment.

Doreen frowned at her and slowly nodded. "I am talking about Eli."

"That's interesting," she said, with a smile. "My mother spent a lot of time with him."

"And Eli's mother was a regular visitor too, as I understand?"

"Yes," she replied, "and the grandmother, I think."

"What about the father?"

"I don't know anything about the father," she stated, looking at her quizzically. "Surely that's on the birth records."

"It might be, if anybody could tell me what Eli's last name was."

The other woman stared at her, her face scrunching up as she thought about it. "And that's not coming to me either."

"Which is precisely my problem," Doreen confirmed, with a gentle smile. "It seems as if Eli was memorable enough but not his last name."

"And all too often," the other woman added, looking at her pointedly, "it's because the last name either isn't used or they didn't associate the person by their last name."

"Meaning they were divorced or didn't have much contact with him?"

"Certainly those are possibilities, but there could also be a lot of other reasons as well."

Doreen frowned. "Still, I'm more or less stuck until I can get a last name." She looked at her and asked, "I don't suppose you know Mary, his mother? Or Glenda, his grandmother?"

She grimaced, while considering that. "We used to know a Glenda Brikins," she mentioned, "but I can't tell you if that was the same Glenda or not."

Doreen wrote down the name. "I can at least pursue that and see if it gives me what I need. There can't be that many Glendas."

"I really wish I could help you more," the other woman said almost anxiously, as if it were the best thing that had happened to her all day. "However, I don't seem to know anything more."

Doreen provided her name and phone number and suggested, "If it comes to you or if you happen to think of a way that I could find it, just give me a call."

Chapter 18

AND, WITH THAT, Doreen headed back out to her car. She sat in the car for a moment and tasted her coffee, surprised that it was still warm. It wasn't hot, but she still wanted her coffee. So she sat here and drank it for a moment, before starting up the car and heading home. Except home wasn't where she ended up. Somehow she found herself heading up to Rutland and right back to the same park again.

She walked toward the crime scene tape, except most of it had been removed. Just a little bit of it still blew in the wind. She stared at the surroundings and shook her head, wondering why the heck she'd come back here again, yet couldn't seem to help herself. It always bothered her to think of somebody stuck here all these years and how nobody even knew. I mean, as a hiding place went, it wasn't bad. It had taken how many years before anybody knew about the body? And that just made it all that much worse.

As she sat here on a park bench with a sigh, staring around, she realized that some animals had been digging away at the site. She winced. It needed to be filled in and quickly. She called Mack.

"Hey, Doreen," he answered. "What's up?"

"It's more of a question."

"Of course it is," he muttered in a wry tone. "What can I do for you?"

"I was just wondering when the hole in the park would be filled in," she replied, "the grave site, I mean."

"As soon as I have the clearance to do it. I believe we have to set up something with the city."

"Because it seems to me that animals are digging into it a lot more."

"What do you mean?"

"New evidence of digging is all around it."

"Is there?" he asked, sounding distracted. "When did you last see it? And has it been since then?"

"Yes," she confirmed. "I saw it yesterday. Yesterday or the day before, but this is definitely new since then."

"Interesting," he murmured. "Do you have Mugs with you?"

"No, I don't. I came straight from the library. I thought I was going home, then suddenly found myself out here."

"Of course you did. We're all working on the case, you know?"

"I know. I know, and we'll get there."

"Let's hope we get there," Mack said pointedly. "At times we just can't solve everything."

"I understand," she murmured. "I just don't want to see this left like it is. Not only is it more of a hazard for any kids coming to this park but it's hardly how I would like to see anybody's grave treated."

"I'll talk to the city today."

"Good enough," she said, ending the call, wishing she had Mugs with her. She walked over to the grave, sad to see that it was just such a desolate and lost place to leave a loved one, somebody tossed away as if not worth a proper burial. As she stared, she caught sight of something very small, very white. She jumped into the depression and leaned forward for a closer look. And then swore. She immediately phoned Mack back.

"You need to come where I am," she exclaimed, trying to keep her voice from getting too anxious.

"And why is that?" he asked. "You know I'm at work, right?"

"You're at work, yes," she snapped, gritting through her teeth, "but I think I see a finger poking out, near Eli's grave."

Chapter 19

DOREEN WAVED AT Mack as he parked and strode toward her. "You came alone?" she asked, looking around.

"I did. Let's just see what you've got first."

She nodded, not wanting to say anything to him, but really? She should know what a finger bone looked like at this point. Almost as if he realized what she wanted to say, he glanced at her and noted, "Of course, it's also déjà vu."

"Right, at my own house," she noted. As they walked toward the depression, she added, "Maybe it's a good thing I don't have Mugs with me today."

"Why is that?"

As they got there, she pointed down at something on the far side. "How can you even tell what that is?" he muttered.

She jumped into the pit. "It's not very deep, only two feet, I would guess." Then he jumped down beside her. She walked over to where the piece of bone was and said, "Now bend down and take a closer look."

As soon as he did, he put a glove on his hand and brushed away a little bit of the dirt around it, then swore.

When he looked up at her, she nodded. "It's another

body, isn't it?"

"Not necessarily," he stated, trying to mask his face. "It's very possible they just missed a few pieces of Eli."

She frowned at him. "Is that possible? Why didn't I think of that?"

He laughed. "Because you're always looking for the next case."

"Not really," she muttered. "Besides, that makes me sound … ghoulish."

"I'm not saying ghoulish, per se," he muttered, looking at her sideways, "but maybe a little."

She groaned and asked, "Will you just pick it up, or do you want to remove it gently?"

He looked at her, brushed off more dirt and then more and a little more.

She finally stepped closer. "I don't know about you, but, unless the forensic team was extremely lax, this appears to be a second body to me."

He quickly pulled out his phone, took photos, and then called Elizabeth.

"What's up?" she asked, distracted.

"Did you supervise the removal of the bones from the site at the park in Rutland?"

"Yeah, sure I did. You were right there with us."

"I know, but I'm sending you a photo right now." As soon as he sent it, he added, "I'll stay on the line, so let me know when you get it."

Almost immediately she swore.

"Yeah, so the question is, are we talking about more of the same body … or is this another one?"

"It's another one," she stated. "It's not as deteriorated."

"How can you tell?"

"Because I can still see flesh on it," she muttered. "I will be right there. Confirm nobody else is around the area."

"Too late," he said, with a chuckle. "Doreen is the one who called me about it."

"Doreen?" she cried out, and then she groaned. "How come we haven't hired that woman?"

And, with that, she ended the call.

Chapter 20

M ACK SAT WITH Doreen, watching her as she stared off to the side, as Elizabeth and her team worked. Mack noted, "You appear to be deep in thought."

She nodded. "Don't suppose you could get me a few answers to a few questions, could you?"

He frowned at her and asked, "What questions?"

"The senator's daughter."

He nodded. "What about her?"

"What was she doing here?"

"She went to school here."

"But she came back, right? I mean, this visit when she went missing wasn't from her school days, correct?"

"I don't know," he replied. "Is it important?"

"Yes, it is important," she stated.

"You think it's connected?" he asked, looking somewhat startled, then back over at the grave.

"Yes, I think it's connected," she said, keeping an eye on the bones.

Mack frowned. "Connected to Eli? Connected to the senator's daughter?"

She nodded. "But nobody will believe me."

"I don't know about that," he muttered. "It seems to me that everybody believes everything you say these days."

"I don't want that either. I'm just trying to get you the proof, so I know too. But I also need to know why she came back."

"You want to tell me why?"

She looked at him and shook her head. "No, not really."

"Okay, I will attempt to get you a few answers, but it'll have to wait."

She nodded. "I don't think it would have to wait very long."

"Then maybe you need to tell me a little more about what you're thinking," he suggested. "Why would you think that this second body, which we don't even know anything about, is connected?"

She smiled. "I can tell you it's connected, sure. However, I can't prove it."

"Ah, I love hearing those words out of your mouth," he teased, with a grin on his face. She didn't grin back, and his smile fell away. "You're really sure of this, aren't you?"

"Sure? … No. Worried that it is? Yes."

"And yet"—he stared at her—"why *worried* though? Do you think we'll find more bodies?"

"I hope not," she said, "but it is a concern."

"What, that there might be more bodies?" he asked, looking at her in astonishment.

"I would need to know why the senator's daughter was up here first."

Frowning, he went to his emails to see if anything helpful was there. "Not a whole lot in the emails regarding that case."

"I hear you," she said. "So really my question is, why was

that not asked?"

"Because the witnesses would have just replied that she came back up for a visit."

"Right, and what are the chances?" She looked around, lowered her voice, and added, "What are the chances that she came up to visit Eli?"

"Time frame's wrong, at least according to what we know to date," he noted, looking around the site. "And yet she might have known him, I guess."

"What did she do for a job? Would she have crossed paths with him somehow?"

"I don't know," he admitted, staring at her, "but their age discrepancy makes that seem to be a huge stretch."

She nodded. "But if, for some reason, this body turns out to be female, will you consider following up on that?"

"Of course I'll follow up," he confirmed, "if for no other reason than now you've got me wondering."

She laughed. "I need you to do more than wonder though," she added. "I know it seems far-fetched, but ..."

"Yeah, not only far-fetched," he interjected, "but it doesn't help us if we've got two bodies here."

"Actually it does."

He groaned, closed his eyes, and asked, "So, do you want to enlighten me on just how it helps?"

"Because very few people would have known where the first body was buried."

He opened his eyes. "So, you're really thinking it's the same killer."

"I am thinking it's the same killer," she stated sadly.

He shook his head. "Please don't tell me that you thinking you know who did it."

"Pretty sure I know who did it. But again ..."

"But again," he pointed out, "we are leaping way too fast in advance of any facts."

Just then Elizabeth straightened, arched her back in a stretch, then walked over toward them. "You just seem to have a nose for murder."

"I know," Doreen whispered. "So, it's a woman, isn't it?"

Elizabeth stared at Doreen and then slowly nodded. "Are you telling me you know who this is?"

"No, I'm not telling you that," Doreen clarified. "I'm just afraid that I do."

Elizabeth looked from her to Mack and back again. "If you can shorten my process of sorting this out," she added, "that would help."

"You may not like what I'm about to say, but I would suggest that you test the DNA from that finger against the DNA you have from the senator's daughter," Doreen suggested.

Elizabeth's expression thinned, and she nodded. "That I can do. We have all that back at the office." With that, she turned to Mack. "Is there any reason to suspect that we need to keep processing this field?"

Mack snorted, then turned to Doreen and asked, "Doreen, is there any reason to suspect that we need to keep processing the rest of this field?"

She looked down at the open gravesite and frowned. "As far as I know at this time, no. Yet I wasn't expecting to see a second body here either."

"Are you sure?" Elizabeth asked, staring at her, almost disgruntled. "You seem to be a step ahead of all of us, each and every time."

"Don't take it personally," Mack told Elizabeth. "You're

just getting a dose of what we have to deal with all the time. Doreen with all the answers, while the rest of us are beating our heads against a wall."

"And yet I don't have all the answers," Doreen admitted. "I wish I did. Just because I have a working theory doesn't mean I have anything that'll hold up in court. I don't think I have anything at the moment that would make either one of you believe me."

Mack sighed. "I highly suggest you come with me back to the office and tell me exactly what you think you've found here."

"I will," Doreen agreed, "tomorrow. After Elizabeth's done her test."

Elizabeth shrugged. "Normally I would go home and get this stench off me, but now you've got me curious. I'll test it as soon as I get back to the lab." And, with that, she headed back over to the grave site and organized the removal and the loading up of all the bones.

As soon as Elizabeth was gone, Mack turned to Doreen and asked, "Do you want to explain?"

"I'm not sure I can," she said, frowning. "It doesn't quite make sense just yet."

"It never makes sense until we get the final pieces, but, if you would at least explain what you think is going on, maybe we can help you formulate a process."

"Wouldn't that be nice," she muttered. "Let me think about it."

"Doreen," he muttered in frustration.

"I know. I know. I know," she muttered in exasperation, "I'm really not trying to be difficult, Mack."

He rolled his eyes. "The thing is, with you, being difficult seems to come naturally."

She nodded. "I know, and I'm sorry. I appear to be a huge burden in your life."

"Whoa, whoa, whoa now," he cut in. "You don't get to say things like that. You're not a burden and never have been a burden, so stop." He frowned at her. "You really think you know who did it?"

She nodded. "I really think I do."

Chapter 21

DOREEN HAD TO admit she'd more or less raced home then, all to avoid having to answer any questions. Not that she had answers, and that was the problem. What she had was a whole lot more in the way of questions. Yet she still felt fairly strongly about what was going on. Still, she just didn't have any way to prove it, and, without proof, she had nothing. She had nothing but her instincts, and that wouldn't get her very far. Particularly if people still living knew about this crime. And potentially the ones who had been heavily involved.

She went home, waited until she thought the park would be empty, and then returned with Mugs and Goliath both trotting happily on leashes. Thaddeus was tucked under the fall of her hair. She wandered around the grave, staring at it, trying to figure out everything about it, letting all the information roll around in the back of her mind.

Then the same woman she'd seen before stopped to ask, "Are you all right?"

Doreen looked over at Meghan, then smiled and nodded. "I could be all right," Doreen shared, "but it's also been a pretty rough day here."

"Why is that?" Meghan asked. She looked over at the grave and gasped. "Oh no, did somebody desecrate it?"

"No, not really," Doreen clarified. "I found a second body in there today."

Meghan stared at her in shock. "What?" she whispered.

Doreen nodded. "I know that's not what any of us expected, but unfortunately that's what happened."

Meghan shook her head. "No way."

But another note filled her tone, with a little bit of a fearful edge. Doreen nodded. "And, of course, that just means I am even more than a little curious as to what happened."

Meghan shook her head. "We'll never know, since it's been so long ago."

"I don't agree with that," Doreen argued. "I'm hoping that we'll find out exactly what happened to poor Eli."

"You think it was Eli?" she asked, her voice trembling.

Doreen looked at her for a long moment. "Are you sure you don't want to tell me all about it?"

Meghan shook her head. "I don't know anything," she cried out, as she backed up quickly. "I don't know anything at all." And, with that, she tried to run away, but Goliath and Mugs cornered her.

Doreen smiled and said, "They won't hurt you."

"That's not what it looks like," Meghan snapped, as she glared down at the animals. "You shouldn't be allowed to have animals out here," she bellowed, as they circled her.

"The problem is that the animals know you have something you're withholding, and, because of that, they're very interested in what you have to say."

Meghan stared at her and then at the animals. "They can't know that."

"Sure they can. They're animals. They sense these things, knowing a whole lot more about the things that happen in life than we ever give animals credit for," Doreen explained. "I'm not saying that you have anything to do with these deaths."

"I didn't. I didn't," she exclaimed. "I don't know anything about it."

"Oh, but I think you do know something."

"No, I don't," she snapped. "I won't say anything."

"Right, because you might know whoever *did* have something to do with these deaths. I have to admit I've been pretty thin on facts when it comes to clues in this case."

"So why are you bugging me?"

"Because you're one of the clues."

"No, I'm not. I just gave you information about Eli."

"And the fact that you did is wonderful," Doreen noted, "because, with any luck, we will prove who this young man is who was buried here, discarded like garbage for so long. And I'm also hoping we can also now identify who the second body is. The fact that there is a second body," she added, "is maybe something you wondered about too?"

"No, no, no, no, I don't know nothing. I only ever wondered about Eli, and that's because you asked me."

"Sure, I asked you here at this park, which is how a lot of people ended up thinking about who could be here."

"I didn't know it was Eli," she stated, looking at her. "You've got to believe me. I didn't know."

Doreen studied her face for what seemed to be an interminably long moment, and then she nodded.

Meghan cried out, "You have to believe me. I didn't know."

"I'm glad to hear that because I would hate to think that

you did know and that you were okay to let him stay here for so long."

"Do you even know if it's him?" she asked, staring back at the grave and then turning away. "Do we have proof that it's even him? I need to know."

"Proof? No, not yet, but again … we're trying to find DNA in order to test the remains." When Meghan's lips trembled, Doreen added, "Unless, of course, you know somebody who might share that DNA."

She turned to Doreen and shook her head. "No, not really."

"Not really?"

"No, I don't know any family members."

"With the genealogy websites, it probably wouldn't take too much to sort it out," Doreen suggested. "Of course, it'll be faster and easier if we could find somebody local—or at least somebody who knows about this body found here."

"I doubt that anybody will talk," Meghan said. "I mean, why would they? They've gotten away with this for so long."

"Yeah, they may have," Doreen admitted, "but then a lot of people don't want to take these kinds of crimes to their deaths, where they may or may not have to face somebody and be held accountable for it."

Meghan bit her lip.

"And withholding the truth is definitely part of that." Doreen had no clue if it was or it wasn't, and she wasn't sure if she should feel bad for assuming it or not. However, she wanted answers. Right now, all she had was hearsay. "When did she approach you?" Doreen asked her.

Meghan looked at her in shock, then stumbled back a step and asked, "Who, who are you talking about?"

Doreen sighed, patted the bench beside her, and said,

"Come on. Let's just sit."

Meghan collapsed more than sat, as she shook her head. "You can't know. You just can't."

"Why not?" Doreen asked, studying Meghan curiously. "Only so many scenarios work."

She blinked and said, "Really?"

"Yes," Doreen replied. "People always think they are the only ones caught up in a mess, or the only ones who know about something, but unfortunately that's often not true."

Meghan slowly sagged in place. "I don't really know anything."

"I understand," Doreen muttered. "But I do think you know more than you are allowing yourself to consider."

"Because I don't want to consider it," she stated, facing her. "There's no way."

"No way what?"

"No way he would have done this," she declared. Doreen just waited. Meghan bounced to her feet. "I have to go," she said, looking around frantically. "I have to think about this." And she bolted.

Doreen called back, "Don't talk to him directly." Meghan stopped, slowly looked at her, and Doreen shook her head. "Just think about it. … If it's him, he's already killed twice."

Meghan's face turned pure white, and she literally ran away.

Doreen sat here for a long moment, before realizing that Meghan had left her purse behind. Doreen stared down at it, opened it, found her wallet, and pulled out her ID. The photo matched Meghan's face, so it was definitely the same woman. Doreen quickly wrote down her address, returned the ID to its slot. She saw something else as she did this. A business card, noting an upcoming appointment for Meghan. To see her oncologist. With a sigh, Doreen got up. "Come on, Mugs and Goliath. We have to return this."

Her home was only a few blocks away. As Doreen and her animals walked slowly along, she wondered at the sense of having pushed the poor woman. Meghan certainly seemed beyond upset. As Doreen got closer and closer to the address, she realized they were coming up to the same block they had walked multiple times already.

Up ahead, she heard somebody yelling and screaming. Mugs started to cry out and whine, pulling on the leash.

She picked up the pace and raced toward the noise, but suddenly all went quiet. She frowned, then turned and looked around, but she heard nothing, absolutely nothing. She saw no people, no sign of anything. She looked down at Mugs. He sniffed the air, then sniffed the ground around him, as if looking for a place to pee. Sure enough, he lifted his leg and emptied his bladder on some poor dandelion that was still probably frozen from the winter weather.

She stared down at Mugs and shook her head. "If only you could talk, buddy."

He gave a *woof*, as if to say it was a good thing he couldn't. Then she led him back to the car. He may not be able to talk, but something was going on, and that something would be beyond ugly. All she had to do was figure it out before someone else died.

Chapter 22

RATHER THAN CONTINUING to walk in the frigid winter air, Doreen headed back to the car and loaded up the animals, plugged the address into the GPS on her phone, found Meghan's home was very close by and headed there. Almost as soon as she got there, the door opened, and Meghan stared at her in shock, as if she were just leaving again.

Doreen held up Meghan's purse. "You left this behind." Meghan snatched it away and clutched it to her chest in relief. "I'm sorry," Doreen added, "that I didn't notice fast enough to stop you."

"No, that's okay." She tried to shut the door in Doreen's face and muttered, "Thank you, thank you."

Doreen nodded. "Remember what I said."

But the door was shut firmly in her face, and with that and the name of this woman, Doreen headed back home again. She'd barely pulled into her driveway, when Mack pulled up behind her. She wasn't sure she was ready to talk to him. Yet he would definitely be brimming over with curiosity. As he unloaded groceries, she realized it was his turn to cook. Immediately her stomach rumbled.

He laughed. "That's a good sign."

"Except that it sees you and starts to rumble," she noted. "It's almost as if my stomach has this vision in its head that *Mack* means *food*."

"Maybe it does," he agreed, with a smile as he looked at her. Then he frowned and asked, "Not a good day at all?"

"Not a perfect day."

He asked, "More puzzle pieces?"

"More puzzle pieces." She nodded. "That's for sure."

"And you're still not ready to share?"

She winced. "No, not really."

"Okay," he replied. "I'm ready when you are. I haven't told the captain because, as soon as I do, he'll want you in the station."

"I know."

"You could give me a hint though," he suggested, turning to look at her.

"I could. Did you get me the answers from the senator?"

"Haven't heard back yet," he replied. "I did email him the questions though."

"He's probably wondering what your problem is, and, after all this time, why you're asking these questions now."

"It makes sense to ask the questions now," he declared, turning to unload the groceries. "Obviously we have to start fresh again, well, … depending on what we found today. I also need to know why that body wasn't found in the first place."

"You never brought the K9s, did you?"

"Not initially, no. But when we did and they signaled. So we dug, found the body, and that was it," Mack explained.

"So, even if there had been a second body buried with

the first one," she said, "it wouldn't have made any difference to the dogs because it wouldn't have been picked up?"

"Maybe," he admitted. "We would hope that maybe we could have found the second one at the same time."

"And maybe you did, but maybe nobody interpreted the K9 signals correctly."

He smiled at her. "Of course, you don't want the dogs to be blamed."

"Of course not," she stated. "They did their jobs, but that doesn't mean that their handlers picked up on it correctly. That's a whole different story."

He laughed. "And anything that gives the dogs some leeway to be free and clear, you're good with."

"Of course, they did their stuff," she said, with a shrug. "It's up to you guys to deal with the rest of it."

He just shook his head and smiled at her. "I'm glad you're so loyal to the animals."

"Somebody has to be." As she sat down at her kitchen table, she asked, "What are we having to eat?"

"I've got chicken breasts here," he replied, "and a dish I want to try."

"Oh, good."

"What about you?" he asked, smiling at her. "Do you want to help? Do you want to learn, or do you want to just relax?"

She frowned at him. "Would you mind if I just … tag along? I need to let my brain shift some things around."

"Not a problem," he said, "as long as you pop up with some answers, at least some of the time, I'm good."

She smiled. "I really do appreciate you. You know that, right?"

He turned to her and smiled right back. "That's one of

the nicest things anybody's ever said to me."

"Oh, I think lots of people say nice things to you," she countered. "You may not listen though."

He burst out laughing. "You could be right. I mean, you absolutely could be right, but I would like to think I have a little more awareness than that."

She just smiled and nodded. With that, she walked into the living room. With Mugs and Goliath and Thaddeus at her side, she stretched out a blanket on the floor in the living room, lying down on top of it, and just let herself relax.

There was just something about this case. She kept trying to make everything fit the facts, and yet what she really needed to do was have the facts fit the case. She wasn't sure when she'd drifted in and drifted out, but suddenly Mack was staring down at her, looking puzzled, asking if she was okay.

"They are connected," she stated. He just nodded and waited. "I need those answers," she repeated, as she slowly sat up.

"And I'll get those answers," he replied, "as soon as I can."

"*Right,*" she muttered, as she looked over at the animals. "What I don't know is what the trigger was."

"But you think you know who and why?"

"Yes, but that doesn't mean I actually have the correct *who.*" When he blinked several times, she shrugged. "I know. It's confusing."

"Darling, your life is confusing," he declared, with a laugh, "but we usually get there eventually."

"We do get there eventually," she stated, "and, in this case, it's a little more confusing but not in a bad way."

"Right, and that's just as confusing," he pointed out,

with a laugh.

"I don't mean it to be."

"Of course you don't," he muttered, with a smile. "And that just makes it even more so."

She groaned. "I know, sorry about that."

"You want to give me a hint?"

"Just that … I think the same person killed both."

He looked at her and nodded. "It would make sense."

"It does, doesn't it? Right. … I mean, how else would he have known where the one body was?"

"You don't think it was accidental?"

"Nope, I don't think so. What I don't understand is why the killer felt it was necessary to take out the second victim."

"Except you do know why," he stated carefully, "because it's the same issue we run into all the time."

She looked at him and nodded. "Because he was afraid of being exposed."

"Exactly," he said. "The only reason for taking out another person is if your secret is about to be exposed."

"So, what possible reason would connect Eli to the senator's daughter?"

"Which we don't know if the second body is the senator's daughter yet. For that matter, we're not sure the first body is Eli."

"Or another woman," she corrected, "to have found out about Eli."

"Maybe she was digging there," Mack guessed, with a shrug. "Maybe it's as harmless as that."

"Maybe," she muttered, giving him a gentle smile. "I highly suspect it was much more emotional than that." He frowned at her. She noted, "Eli had a brain tumor, but nobody ever said that he was actually"—she floundered for words—"mentally disabled? Is that the word?"

"Something along that line, yes."

"And just because he had a brain tumor, and he obviously had some issues, that doesn't mean that somebody else might not have either really liked him or had some feelings for him."

"And that's possible. We're still talking about a big difference of many years though, if you're thinking the senator's daughter had a thing for Eli."

"And I wondered about that. So, if she was that much younger, the only way she would have known about Eli would be through somebody who connected the two of them."

He sat down in the living room with her. "So you think that somebody who either worked with or otherwise knew Eli had a connection to the senator's daughter—or some other woman."

Doreen nodded. "I'm thinking so."

"Sure, but that could be anybody. Could be a nurse, could be a doctor, could be a caregiver, could be anybody along that line. … What is this then? Some caregiver's daughter was buried near Eli?" After a moment, he added, "But if the second body is potentially the senator's daughter, I don't think she was a caregiver at any time in her short life."

"Right," Doreen agreed, staring at him. "So, where did the senator's daughter stay when she was here visiting?"

"I'm not sure." He frowned. "That's another good question. It goes to show how incomplete the files are. All I have is that she went missing from the Kelowna area."

"Sure, but the Kelowna area is massive."

"Which includes Rutland, where her body may have just

been found. So why would she have gone up to Rutland?"

"Yet, if her friends were there, or if she was caught up in a mystery up there, she could have gone to Rutland. It is possible."

"Maybe she came to see some friends," he suggested, trying to steer her around, "because she went to school here."

"Okay, so somebody her age somehow connected her with somebody who knew about Eli because it's the only thing that makes sense," Doreen cried out. "The only reason for the senator's daughter to be in basically the same grave as Eli is if somebody was trying to keep the two of them … apart—or maybe keep the two of them together."

"What are you thinking?" Mack asked, frowning.

"Burying them together was to keep it secret," she theorized. "And, in the killer's mind, they might as well be together."

"Why would he say that?"

"The only reason he would say that," she replied, "is because she was either poking her nose into Eli's disappearance or in some way making the killer feel threatened. And to feel threatened meant that he knew her, knew about her, or in some way found out about her."

"And again, speculation, … and possible theories won't get us far," he pointed out. "I can see that the same person killed them both, and the two bodies could have absolutely nothing to do with each other, except for the fact that, if one were found, the second would be too. Yet, with the first body not found in all these years, maybe he just thought that reopening the grave to bury the second body was a great hiding place."

"Why though?" she asked. When Mack didn't respond immediately, she asked, "The grave for the female … wasn't as deep, was it?"

"No, it wasn't," he confirmed, with a smile. "I wondered if you would recognize that. His was much deeper, which just means that the other body was buried afterward, which we already know. Even if it isn't the senator's daughter," he noted, "we do know it was buried afterward. It's also not as decomposed. So each body could fit the broad age parameters for when Eli and then later the senator's daughter went missing."

"Right," she muttered. "But what do they have in common, and how would their paths have crossed?"

"You realize that their paths didn't have to cross, right? It could just have easily been that she crossed paths with the killer. So, not knowing what else to do but having drawn on the success of his first murder, he took out the second one."

She nodded. "I don't like that theory, but it does work."

He made a mock bow from his sitting position. "Thank you," he said, dipping his head. "I do appreciate the confidence."

She rolled her eyes. "I mean, you are a cop."

"Thank you," he quipped, "thank you for recognizing that."

She burst out laughing, gave him a big hug, and then announced, "I'm hungry."

THE NEXT MORNING Doreen slept in. It hadn't been a great night. She kept waking up, thinking about the two cases, then going back under, but she just couldn't see any scenario that made sense to her. As soon as she got up, made coffee, poured her first cup, and basically collapsed onto her chair at the kitchen table, yawning, her phone rang. She groaned, thinking there was a lot to be said for nobody knowing who she was or where she lived or what her phone number was, since it kept everybody out of her face. But the police station was calling, so she answered, only to find the captain on the other end.

"Doreen, Mack says you have a working theory."

"He might have jumped the gun a little bit on that," she clarified. "I might have a theory. I'm not sure it's working."

He burst out laughing. "Welcome to police work."

She muttered, "If only people would just tell the truth."

"But they don't want to," he said, with a snort. "That's just a fact of life."

"I know, and it's frustrating," she muttered. "I mean, all kinds of things would be settled in no time if people would just open up and talk."

"Isn't that the truth?" he muttered. "So, do you want to come in and talk to us?"

"I don't really have anything for you," she said cautiously.

"We don't have much either. Yet apparently you're the one who already pinpointed that this could be the senator's daughter," he explained. "So why don't you come in and sort that one out for us?"

It's not as if he was giving her any option. "Fine," she muttered, "but I'm telling you upfront, I don't really have any answers."

"I'll take what you've got," he said, "because, right now, you've got more than we do."

"You guys would get here on your own," she added.

"We didn't though, so get your butt in here. I'll even make sure there's coffee for you."

She laughed. "But then again, it'll be, you know, … *cop coffee.*"

"Which is good enough for us," he declared. "And you're almost one of us at this point in time, so it should be good enough for you too."

"And I can bring the animals?"

"Of course you can bring the animals," he said in exasperation. "I don't think I've ever known you *not* to have them with you."

With that and a smile on her face, she sent Mack a text, saying that she'd been summoned. He sent her a thumbs up, followed by **Good luck.** She wasn't sure what that meant. Stopping long enough to load up the animals, she stuffed her pockets full of treats to help all of them behave, should this meeting be too long and too busy to pay them any attention. As she was about to step out, Nan called.

"Wow," Nan greeted her. "Where are you off to?"

"How do you know that I'm off to somewhere?" she asked, staring down at her phone, puzzled.

"You're huffing and puffing. Good Lord, that can't be good."

"No, it sure can't be," she muttered, not getting into it. "So, what did you find out? I'm still looking for answers. Did you guys come up with anything?"

"We think we have a couple people who potentially have a link to Eli's family."

"Oh good," she said. "Are they here? Can I talk to them this morning? I really want to have something in terms of an answer to give to the captain."

"The captain?" Nan repeated, seemingly thrilled.

"Yes, he just called, and I've been summoned, as I've just told Mack. But being summoned doesn't mean I have any answers."

"No, it sure doesn't," Nan exclaimed, yet still excited. "It is nice to think that you're being summoned."

"Yeah, says you," Doreen muttered, "but I would feel better if I had something to give them."

"Come down now if you want. I'm expecting to talk to Sally here in the next little bit."

"And who is Sally?"

"We believe she knew Glenda."

"Okay, I'm on my way."

Chapter 24

ONCE IN THE car, Doreen made a quick adjustment to her schedule and headed to Nan instead. As she pulled up to the front of Rosemoor, she was hoping that the whole gang hadn't arrived yet at Nan's apartment.

And, sure enough, as she got there, Nan confirmed, "You made it before everybody else."

"Is Sally here?"

"Yes, Sally is here," she said, and, with that, she led the way into the living room.

Doreen walked over and sat down in front of the older lady, who was looking a little nervous. "Hi, I'm Doreen."

The woman looked thrilled at that, clapping her hands together. "Oh my. I do hope I have some good information for you."

"I hope you do too," Doreen replied, "but I'll take the truth. Whatever it is that you've got, let's not embellish it, just speak the truth."

"Oh, no problem there," she stated, with a nod. "I don't deal in half-truths, and I certainly don't believe in lies, not like everybody in today's world," she declared, with a hard look over at Nan.

Doreen wasn't sure exactly what that was about, but she sidelined it very quickly and replied, "Good, so could you tell me about Glenda? So far, you're the only person who I've found to have known Glenda."

"I knew a Glenda," she clarified, "though I don't know if it's the same one or not. But she worked in the kitchen at one of the mental health homes."

"Interesting," Doreen noted, "so that certainly could be the Glenda I'm interested in." Sally looked thrilled. "Do you know anything about her family?" Doreen asked.

"Oh yes," Sally said. "She worked partly to help with her grandson's upkeep, but then she had to retire, and her daughter was working as a cleaner. I believe her daughter's son was there, so she kept working as long as she could, but then the rules changed or something. I don't quite understand how that worked, you know, how the government can come and take all those innocent souls and just kick them out into the street."

"I'm not exactly sure how that worked either," Doreen agreed. "Do you know what Glenda's last name was?"

"Woodstock."

Doreen wrote that down with relief. "So, her daughter would have been?"

"Mary Woodstock, but she married."

"Who did she marry?"

"I don't know what his name was." She pondered that. "I think it was … I'm not sure. I wouldn't want to give you a name and have it be wrong."

"If you give me a name, at least I can check it out. If it's wrong, then I don't go forward. However, if I don't have a name, I can't even check it out."

"I suppose that makes sense," Sally conceded, but she

sounded very unsure.

"How about a first name?" Doreen asked. "Do you know what the husband's first name is?"

"Yes, it was something weird, like Cody, I think."

Doreen didn't think Cody was a very strange name but to each their own. "Okay, so Cody, and then we just need the last name."

Sally frowned, thought about it, and shook her head. "It was something funny, but I'm not sure it's the name he always went by."

At that, Doreen stopped and looked at her. "Most people have a surname they go by all the time."

"Yes, yes, I know. However, I'm thinking that, in the divorce, there was something about names."

"Oh, so they were divorced?" Doreen asked.

"Oh yes," Sally muttered. "I think it was the young man's health issues that brought about the divorce."

"And did the father ever have anything to do with him?"

"I wouldn't know," she said. "But, if they're divorced, that doesn't mean he doesn't still have something to do with his son."

"No, of course not. And the grandmother, Glenda, is she still alive?"

"No, no, she's not. She's been gone quite a few years now," Sally replied.

"What about the daughter, Mary? I believe she was supposed to have died of cancer."

Sally frowned at Doreen. "I'm not sure about the daughter. I haven't seen her in quite a while so that's possible."

"Okay," she muttered. "Did the daughter have any identifying marks or did she have any other family?"

"It's Eli you're trying to find?" Sally asked.

"Yes," she answered, as something else started to sink into her brain. "Was any other family in town?"

Sally grimaced. "I don't think so. Last I heard, … I think the father lived down at the coast. I thought there was something about Eli going off to the coast too."

"Good enough." Doreen nodded, then turned to Nan. "I can look up Woodstock and see if we come up with any matches on that."

Sally clapped again. "That would be lovely if you could, and, please, let me know if any of the information I gave you has helped."

"I will indeed," Doreen stated, as she looked back at the two other people now here. "What I really could use is a family member to speak with, or a last name."

Sally shrugged, but one of the others raised a hand. "Oh, I think there was another child. Eli had a sibling."

"Right, and that's the child I need to find," Doreen said, trying not to push, but feeling desperate for the information. "Boy or girl?"

"Girl," she replied instinctively, and then laughed. "But I don't know why or how I would even know that."

"Of course, but Woodstock as a last name would be a help. Of course it's the Grandma's last name, not the kids'." Doreen told Nan, "Gotta run."

Nan nodded, then smiled. "Good luck."

"Yeah, *right*," Doreen muttered. As she got to the police station, she parked outside, and, before she went in, she called Elizabeth Harley, the coroner.

"Haven't got the results back yet," Elizabeth said.

"Okay, I have another person you need to test DNA against. If it's in the database, I mean."

"Who're you thinking?"

"I'm thinking the young man who was in there with the female's body."

A moment of silence followed, and then Elizabeth asked, "You think the two bodies buried in the same place are related?"

"I'm afraid now that they may be mother and son, or possibly siblings," she shared. "I just don't know for sure yet."

"That's what DNA is for," Elizabeth said. "I'll run it, but no guarantee how long it'll take."

"I understand."

"But now you've got me going, so I'll do this as fast as I can. Hopefully I can get preliminary findings through fairly quickly."

"I'm heading into the police department now," Doreen added.

"Oh, why is that?" Elizabeth asked.

"It seems the captain wants to talk to me," she replied. "I have two theories now, and I just don't have a way to prove which one it is."

"So work on one, and, if it doesn't work, look to the other theory."

"I know," Doreen said, with a laugh. "Yet that doesn't necessarily mean I'll find the answers very quickly."

"No, of course not."

As Doreen opened her car door, she tried to figure out why the name *Woodstock* was sticking in her throat. Then she remembered. She stopped, gasping, as she turned on her phone and pulled out the woman's name that she had found in the purse at the park. Then she called her. As soon as the woman answered, she said, "Hi, this is Doreen. I need to talk to you about the Woodstock family."

"Oh my gosh," the woman cried out. "You do know."

"I don't know if I know or not," Doreen acknowledged, "but what I need is for you to tell me the truth."

"And I'll tell you the truth," she whispered, her voice trembling, "but not over the phone. Not like this."

"Okay, how about I come pick you up?" Doreen offered. "I'm supposed to speak to the captain about all this, but I need to know the truth first."

"I understand," Meghan muttered.

"Do you want to come to the police station with me?" Doreen asked her.

"No, no, no," she replied, sounding frantic. "I don't want anything to do with the police," she cried out. "If you'll make me do that, I won't talk to you."

"I won't make you do that," Doreen declared, "but, Meghan, we do need answers."

"Yes, yes, it's time."

"Particularly when I know you're not in great health."

Meghan sighed. "No, I'm not, and somehow it doesn't surprise me that you know that too."

"I do know that there is one chance to clear up some wrongs," Doreen shared, "so let's sort that out first."

"Yes, of course."

Doreen added, "I'll meet you at the park in, say, … ten minutes. I'm already driving. Be there soon."

She called the captain, couldn't get him, so she called Mack and shared, "Mack, I'm heading to the park first. I may have more answers than I thought, but I need to confirm something." And then she ended the call, not giving him a chance to answer.

Turning her vehicle around, she headed straight for the park. If nothing else, maybe today something would go her way, and Doreen would finally get answers for poor Eli. She suspected it would leave a lot more blanks about something else, but she could only deal with one case at a time. And Elizabeth was right. If Doreen could solve one of these cases, then she knew exactly what her next cold case would be.

As she headed down the road, Mack called her back.

"Hey," she answered. "Can't talk right now. I'm just pulling into the parking lot. But can you see if any Woodstocks are left in town?"

"Woodstocks?" he repeated. "Are you serious? There's probably a half dozen."

"Yeah, but are any at …" And she gave him the address.

"Just a minute," he said in frustration. "One of these days, you'll learn to be a team player."

"Not today," she quipped, then laughed. "Actually it is today, because you're the one who's helping me out."

"Yeah, but remember that it's supposed to be the other way around."

"*Cold case*," she noted, "definitely my territory."

"We're supposed to be working together. So, maybe *you* need to work together. So … Woodstock. … Yes, there is one at that address. … Wait. I know where that is."

She laughed. "Yeah, you sure do." And, with that, she ended the call, pulled into the parking lot, and stepped out to see Meghan standing in the park, staring down at the grave.

Doreen walked over to her and smiled. "So, are you ready to tell us what happened to poor Eli and his mother? Or was it Eli and his sister?"

Meghan frowned at her, then looked down at the grave and whispered, "It's not my story to tell."

"Maybe not," Doreen admitted, "but, if it isn't your story to tell, whose is it?"

At that came a gnarly voice behind them. She turned to face the older man that they had seen here on the very first day, and she nodded. "Hello, Mr. Woodstock. Presumably this is your story."

He glared at her and grumbled, "You're nothing but a troublemaker."

"And I might be," she agreed. "However, an awful lot of people deserve better than this." She motioned at the grave in front of her.

"Maybe, but back then there weren't many options," he stated.

His wife was at his side, trembling in the cold.

Looking over at her, Doreen asked, "Are you all right?"

She shrugged and shook her head. "No, not really."

Doreen nodded. "But still, the truth needs to come out."

"Does it?" she whispered. "I'm not so sure about that."

Chapter 25

DOREEN STARED AT the married couple, Meghan standing quietly just off to the side. Doreen added, "If you had something to do with this, we need to know." She was hoping to solve a case that was easy for a change.

"No, you don't," the old man snapped, glaring at her. "We didn't have anything to do with any of this. How could you even think that?" he cried out.

She sighed. Nope, this one didn't appear to be headed toward *easy* at the moment.

The older couple stared at the grave and shook their heads. The wife said, "This wasn't us. We don't know who it was, but it wasn't us."

Doreen groaned. "If it wasn't you guys, how come you know about it?"

"We didn't know about it, but, as soon as you opened it, we worried that we might know," the wife admitted. "Particularly when you mentioned he was so tall."

"If it wasn't you, and it wasn't you, and it wasn't you," she noted, looking at all three of them, "how come you all seem to know something?"

"No," replied Meghan, despite telling Doreen that she

wanted to talk now. "We don't know. That's the problem. You're looking for answers, and we can't help you."

Doreen stared at her in frustration. "So why did you call me out here?"

"Because I wanted you to talk with us but not make accusations."

"I'm not accusing anybody," Doreen stated, trying hard to suppress a scream. "But you're darn frustrating."

"That's because you're trying to fit the crime to us, and we didn't do it," Meghan pointed out.

Doreen groaned because that was exactly what Mack would say she was doing. "Fine," she muttered. "Who do you think did this?" When they all shook their heads in silence, she stared at them. "Not one of you is willing to give up a name?"

"That's because we don't know," the wife said.

Doreen sighed. "You wouldn't tell me even if you do know."

"We don't know," Mr. Woodstock snapped.

Doreen nodded. "Fine," she muttered, raising both hands. "But, if you do know, and I find out afterward that you knew, it won't be helpful, and it will lead to obstruction of justice charges."

"It was so long ago," wailed the wife, trembling in the cold. "It could have been anything."

"But it wasn't anything," Doreen declared, staring at her, "and you and I both know that."

She nodded and shrugged. "Sure, but we didn't know what was going on either."

"So, why are you all walking around here as if you did something wrong then?"

They looked at each other and groaned. The wife added,

"Because we did do something wrong, but it wasn't to harm another person."

"What do you mean?" Doreen asked, glaring at them. "What did you do wrong?"

The old man grumped, "We don't need to tell you nothing."

"No, you don't," Doreen agreed, "but this is a murder investigation. So, if you're trying to withhold something from us, that's a whole different story."

"Are you acting in an official capacity?" the old man asked, glaring at her.

"Officially, no," she stated, "but I've been called in to report to the captain this morning. Do you want me to tell him to tear apart your life in order to figure out why and what you're hiding?"

Meghan looked at the older couple and suggested, "It can't be that bad, so you should just tell her."

Doreen snorted. "Oh, I don't know how bad anything is because nobody is talking. So, for all I know, it *is* that bad." She frowned at them. "But I can tell you this—it'll be a whole lot worse if we don't find out the truth from you three first."

"You don't know what the truth is. The truth is, nobody ever knows what the truth is," the old guy replied cryptically.

Meghan spoke up. "Look. We all worked at the same home."

Doreen nodded. "Ah, Sky Manor, where Eli was."

The old man nodded. "Yes, way back when, different years, different generations even," he noted, pointing at Meghan.

"There was nothing terribly wrong with Eli," he shared. "I mean, obviously he had some issues with the brain tumor, but he wasn't mentally incapacitated from birth. Still, obviously he'd had a lot of challenges."

Meghan added, "He was a really nice young man."

"Okay, so keep talking," Doreen urged.

The wife interjected, "We don't know what happened to him. He just up and disappeared one day."

"And you didn't report it?" Doreen asked.

The wife shrugged. "We heard that his father came and took him, and he went to the coast."

Doreen frowned. "And yet you don't seem to think that was the truth."

The wife moaned. "We don't know if it was the truth or not. We're worried that it wasn't the truth, particularly now that you found a body here."

She nodded. "And I'm looking for Eli's family. The Woodstocks, I believe."

"We don't know anything much of the family," the old guy grumbled. "His mother came all the time, but I don't know what happened to her either."

"Right, but you do know that we just found a second body, right?"

He paled and started to shake. "No, no, no," he yelled, throwing his hands around, flailing. "That wasn't us."

Doreen continued. "So far, we have two bodies, and we're not exactly sure who is involved. What we do know is people are not talking."

The old guy snapped, "Of course they are not talking. Not when you come in here and start accusing people."

She stared at him. "I haven't accused anybody. But if you want me to start, I'm happy to."

He snorted. "Your type is all the same."

"Hardly," she declared. "I'm at least talking to you. You

do know that, when the police come, they'll step into your house with a warrant, and they'll tear the house apart and then tear apart your life. And they'll do the same with you." Doreen pointed at his wife.

At that, Mrs. Woodstock cried out, "No, please, please, we don't have much."

"Maybe you don't," Doreen said, "but obviously you know something that you're keeping secret."

Mrs. Woodstock looked over at her husband, then back at Doreen and shared, "Look. What we did was wrong, but it wasn't *killing* wrong."

"Wrong, but not killing wrong?" Doreen repeated, as she assessed the three of them. "What did you do?"

Meghan said, "It probably doesn't even mean anything, but chances are it would lead to this."

"Yes, it would," Doreen replied, getting frustrated. The animals wandered around, sniffing all around the old man. She looked down at Mugs and muttered, "Mugs, you're not being terribly nice. Come over here."

But Mugs wasn't moving. He kept sniffing at the old man's legs.

The old man glared at him. "Get that dog away from me," he cried out. "Get him away." And he started kicking at Mugs.

Mugs backed up so that he was at least out of kicking range, and then he sat and looked up at him.

The old man yelled, "I'm not staying here another minute. You tell her. I'm going home." And, with that, he turned and stomped off. The trouble was, he was old and his stomping-off level was pretty anticlimactic.

Doreen watched him go, then turned back to the two women. "You want to explain that?"

"It's your dog for one thing," the wife pointed out. "He has a catheter bag, so the dog can probably smell it."

"Of course," Doreen said, looking down at Mugs regretfully. "That might not have been well done on your part," she muttered to Mugs.

He just sat and looked up at Doreen.

The wife continued. "He is just a dog, but Welford is on his last legs. I know something's been bothering him, but he won't talk to me about it," she complained. "So he just keeps getting more and more upset about this grave here."

"I'm sure he is upset," Doreen conceded, "but somebody needs to open up. You say that these dead bodies have nothing to do with you."

"No, they don't," Mrs. Woodstock stated, "but I think he's afraid he might know who it is."

"Can you get him to talk to me about it, because Welford certainly won't like it when the police come."

"No, he won't like that at all." The wife sighed. "Can you give me an extra day, just to see if I can get him to open up?"

Doreen shook her head. "The police want answers today. Tomorrow is not likely." Doreen turned to Meghan. "What about you? Do you know any more about this mess that's going on?"

She shook her head. "No, I don't."

"So, what is it you were going to tell me about today?"

Meghan winced, nodded at the older woman, and replied, "I would point out that they might have had something to do with it." When the old woman stared at her in shock, Meghan shrugged. "You're always out here. You're always haunting this place, as if it's got the answers to some secret."

The older woman flushed and admitted, "I told him that we shouldn't be quite so obvious, but he wouldn't listen, and he's desperate."

"Desperate for what?" Doreen asked.

Mrs. Woodstock groaned. "Supposedly somebody left a tin can out here, full of diamonds and jewels."

Meghan stared at her. "That's what you're after?" she asked. "That's just an old wives' tale."

Doreen looked from one to the other. "Hang on a minute. So you're out here trying to find coins and jewels, and you had nothing to do with the murders?"

"No, we didn't," Mrs. Woodstock replied.

"So, why are you thinking you're in trouble now?" Doreen asked.

The wife winced. "Because Welford thought a body could be here. He had a dog years ago, an old police dog. It kept signaling here, and Welford didn't want to get involved. So we just didn't do anything about it. So now that you've found the body, Welford's afraid that he'll get blamed."

"Good God," Doreen muttered, shaking her head at them. "So, you had nothing to do with any of this?"

"No," Mrs. Woodstock cried out. "Honest. We didn't."

"Did you actually think treasure was buried here?" Doreen asked, incredulous.

"There was talk of treasure, and we're broke," Mrs. Woodstock shared. "Like, really broke. If we don't come up with some funds soon, we'll lose our home," she explained. "It's tearing my husband apart. He doesn't have long to live, but he's worried about me."

"What about a retirement home for you?" Doreen asked, looking at her carefully, not knowing quite what to think. It was just a silly-enough excuse to be the truth. However, that was an awful lot of cloak-and-dagger stuff for them to be involved in and to have nothing to show for it. "And you're telling me that, in all the years you lived by this park, you never found the pot of gold?"

"No," she replied, shrugging. "In a way we just gave up. But we can't stop walking here, partly because we know there's a body."

Doreen let her breath out in a hard gush. "So much for that theory. The crazy stuff that people do."

"I know. I know," Mrs. Woodstock whispered.

"And you're honestly telling me that you're not criminally involved in any of this? If there is some crime to confess, now would be the time to tell."

"No, no, no, no, no." Then she frowned at Doreen. "Isn't it enough that we let that poor man remain here all these years?"

"More than that," Doreen spelled out, "the chance to make somebody pay for this and to bring closure to a family was also denied. That's something that you will have to answer to the police about."

She paled but nodded. "That we can do," she muttered.

"Even if you just tell them that you didn't know for sure what the dog was signaling," Meghan suggested. When she got a glare from Doreen, Meghan grimaced. "I'm sorry. I thought they might have had something else to do with this."

Doreen nodded, still not exactly sure how much of this was truth versus fiction. "Have you ever heard anything about a pot of gold being stashed here?"

"No, not at all," Meghan said. Then she turned and eyed the old woman suspiciously. "If it was here, I suspect it would have been found by now."

The older woman shrugged. "We never heard anybody say anything about finding it."

"Whose was it?"

The wife paled, pinched her lips, then she sighed.

"Are you telling me it was Eli's?" Doreen asked.

She shrugged.

"Did you know Eli was lying here?" Doreen pressed on.

She didn't say anything more.

"Good God," Doreen cried out. "So, not only did nobody have the proper respect to bury this poor man, you didn't have the respect to see that the crime against him was taken care of by the police so the guilty party would pay a price for having done this to him. Plus, Eli would get a proper burial."

The wife just stared at her.

Doreen snorted. "I'm not sure I believe any of this at the moment," she muttered. "I will be taking this all up with the captain."

The wife nodded. "We might not be sterling people," she snapped, "but we were just trying to stay out of trouble."

"Stay out of trouble? You knew that somebody was buried here all these years," Doreen pointed out, "and all you can say is you wanted to stay out of trouble?"

It was the first time in a long time that Doreen had felt that level of disgust. Even Mugs seemed to feel pretty strongly about it. He barked several times at Doreen, who looked down at him and nodded. "I know, buddy. It's pretty bad, isn't it?" She turned to face Mrs. Woodstock. "Does your husband even have a catheter bag, or is that just his way of running away from his responsibility and his guilt?"

"It was his way of running," she admitted, "but I also knew that it would cause the dog to react the way he did."

"In other words you're smart enough to say something to get him off, so he can walk away and not get blamed for anything. So, is he at home right now, packing up your stuff?"

"No," she stated, showing her palms. "We're way too old to run."

"So, you say. I just have to wonder if anything else was going on in all this time."

Mrs. Woodstock pinched her lips together. "We told you what we know. You'll do what you will with that information." And, with that, she turned and moved semirapidly in the direction her husband had gone.

Doreen turned to Meghan.

The other woman shrugged and muttered, "I don't know what to say to that one."

"And yet you didn't want to tell me either," Doreen noted.

"Not for that reason," she clarified, shaking her head. "I just didn't want to turn in two old people to the police if there wasn't any just cause. How could I do that?" she muttered.

"Are you related to them, what with your last name also being Woodstock?" Doreen asked.

"No," she said. "We often thought that we might be related because we have the surname in common, or thought we did, but it just didn't happen to be that way. For a while, we tried to follow the family trees, thinking that it was just fun. Eventually we gave it up. Now we probably could do one of those DNA ancestry things and see if there is a connection somewhere," she muttered. "I don't think anybody cares at this point. They're too old and are just trying to make themselves comfortable in their final years."

"Maybe so, but there are also homes for them to retire in," Doreen noted, "as they well know. They won't be on the street, not here, not in Canada."

Meghan nodded. "I don't have a clue what else they would be up to, but I don't think in my heart of hearts they had anything to do with this. As much as I might like to see them pay the price for having not pitched in and helped out on a crime that somebody could have some closure on, maybe they figured it didn't matter. I mean, if you think about it. I don't know if anybody in Eli's family is even left alive to care about him."

"Maybe," Doreen muttered, staring in the direction the older couple had gone. "I think the whole thing is shaky, including their explanations."

As she drove back to the police station, she realized she had absolutely nothing to share, and what she did have was beyond silly. As she walked into the police station, they all looked at her and asked, "You got it solved?"

"I thought I was getting somewhere," she muttered, "but apparently I'm nowhere."

"Ha, welcome to our world," the captain replied, as she wandered in. "Glad you finally made it."

"I went to talk to somebody who I thought had something to do with it, and you still need to look into this, just see if you want to pursue it or not." Then she told them the sad tale.

"Good God." The captain frowned.

"Yep, Welford had a dog that supposedly was a police dog, and it signaled to a body there, and they said nothing about it to anyone. That's the story according to them because they were looking to find whatever treasure supposedly was buried in the park." As they all just frowned at each other, she nodded. "Dodgy, I know."

"Yeah, you're not kidding," the captain muttered. He got their contact information from Doreen and announced, "I guess somebody needs to go talk to them."

Mack offered, "I will."

"Good," Doreen agreed. "They're definitely a unique couple."

"And we will take that into account," the captain muttered.

Doreen added, "They're also likely to say they didn't have any idea what the dog could do, so they didn't really understand until the grave was opened."

"Of course they will," the captain grumbled, with a headshake. "Anything to keep their butts out of trouble." He looked at her and asked, "So, what will you do now?"

"It's all so dodgy," she repeated. "It makes no sense with these answers, and that's all I can say. We're still waiting for the DNA. I may know more then."

"That's right. We are," the captain noted, "and hopefully that will come up with something."

"Plus," Doreen added, "did Elizabeth come up with a better idea of how Eli died?"

Just then the door to the office opened, and Elizabeth walked in. She looked at Doreen and asked, "Did they finally give you a desk here?"

"No, not at all," she said, with a smile.

"Maybe they should." She dropped the file into the captain's hands. "She was right. It's familial DNA."

"Mother or sister?" Doreen turned to look at her.

The coroner turned to Doreen and shook her head. "That was an interesting twist too. You are just full of victims, aren't you?"

"I'm afraid I am," Doreen muttered, slowly straightening. "So, you want to give me the answer to that story?"

Elizabeth smiled. "Sister."

Doreen looked around the room at all the faces, confusion and shock filling their expressions, but all she could say was, "Gotcha."

Chapter 26

MACK GROANED. "DOREEN, you can't just stay at home. Everybody wants answers."

"They can have answers as soon as I get them."

"You said *gotcha* and then raced out of the office," Mack said in frustration. "I don't believe that you're being theatrical on purpose, but people need to know what's going on."

"That's what I'm trying to figure out," she told him.

"So, are you not exactly sure? I mean, what was that *gotcha* if you didn't have it all figured out?"

"The *gotcha* was that I had guessed right," she explained. "The *gotcha* was because I'm on the path. I just don't quite have the right answers yet. That's the problem. I want to get those answers before I have to explain to everybody what's going on. Now," she added, with a snort, "we have a last name. Can you check to see if there happens to be an Eli who's alive?"

"An Eli Woodstock?" Mack asked.

"Well, his Grandmother was a Woodstock…"

Then Mack cursed.

"Now what?" she asked.

"What if the mother didn't die of cancer and actually

remarried?"

"Yes, that could work too."

"Yes, let me check to see what I can rustle up." He groaned. "I want answers, and I want them fast."

"Me too," she muttered, "and I know time's running out."

"No, time's not really running out," he argued. "I highly doubt anybody else will die in this. However, we already have the two bodies, Eli and his sister. So what about the senator's daughter?"

"This apparently doesn't have anything to do with her," she conceded. "I was wrong on that."

"Okay, because the captain will make that case a priority."

"He can make it a priority after we solve this one," she muttered.

Mack snorted. "You know it doesn't work like that, right? He's got people to keep happy, and senators tend to come above the common folk."

"They shouldn't," she snapped.

"Easy now," he muttered. "I know that you're getting stressed out, and I need to know that you're okay."

She took a deep breath. "I'm okay, but something is going on here, something I don't understand, and it involves all of them."

"All three of them? Meaning all three Woodstocks, the old man, his wife, and Meghan, who isn't related to those two?"

"Yes, I think so. I'm just not sure how."

"Okay," he said, "I will do some research, and I'll get back to you." Then he ended the call.

She smiled, then sent him a text. **Thank you.** And she

added a heart emoji.

He sent back a thumbs-up, and she figured that meant he was still pissed at her. But, being Mack, he wouldn't hold it against her. There was a lot to be said about a man who could move when circumstances required it, and that was definitely him.

As she sat here, going through as much of the internet as she could, she needed Nan's help. "Nan," she greeted her grandmother, as soon as she picked up the phone. "Do you know anybody down on the coast?"

"No, I sure don't," she muttered. "Why?"

"I just wondered if you knew any Woodstocks down that way."

"No, I sure don't. You still haven't figured it out?"

She frowned. "Thanks for the vote of confidence."

"I didn't mean it that way," Nan replied cautiously.

"I know you didn't," she muttered. "I'm just feeling the pressure on this one."

"Just relax. Nobody is expecting you to have this solved today."

As Doreen ended the call, it felt exactly as if she was expected to have it solved today. And that was a problem. She groaned as she looked around her small kitchen, until her gaze landed on Solomon's files again.

She got up and headed over to them. even though she had written the summaries, that didn't mean that she hadn't missed something in all of them. As a matter of fact, she could quite easily have missed quite a bunch.

It was an odd thing to see so many files. She knew that she had put so many in order, but what if she had put something back maybe not quite right. She frowned as she stared at the pile of boxes and then pulled out her printed copy of all the file summaries. Something could be there—something had to be there. Then she went back to the internet and looked for a visual of these people.

She didn't have anything for Eli or his sister and couldn't for the life of her come up with a picture of the mother or the grandmother.

She frowned and called the library. Thankfully she got the librarian she absolutely loved and asked, "Is there any way to get an image of somebody who would have worked at one of the mental health homes or would have been a patient there, over the last thirty years?"

"You could always talk to them about their archives," she suggested. "Images would not be that good necessarily because they probably have been scanned in."

"Right," Doreen noted. "And scanning archives is definitely what they might have done, I guess."

"Absolutely."

"It's hard enough for anybody to handle that level of scanning without it being a professional company."

The librarian pointed out, "It's been a long time ago, and nobody's likely to have any of that information. Plus, that kind of medical data is probably confidential, even down to photographs of patients. Don't quote me though."

"*Right*. What about locals? What about the hospitals? What about ..."

"Whoa, whoa. Who is it that you're looking for?"

"A picture of Eli Woodstock, potentially Woodstock. His mother was born as a Woodstock, and I don't know what her married name would have been. Mack is doing some research on that for me right now."

The librarian pondered that. "A bunch of Woodstocks were in town here."

"I know, and short of hitting the phone books and individually dialing every one of them," Doreen noted, "I'm not exactly sure what I'm supposed to do."

"Did you check the marriage registration?"

"Do you have that there?"

"Sure, I do. Come on down."

And, with that, Doreen raced out of the house, with Mugs barking as she closed the door behind her and bolted down to the library.

"That was fast," the librarian noted, as Doreen raced in.

"Yeah, well, I don't know why, but I just feel as if an awful lot is riding on this."

"In that case," she added, "you'll be happy to know that, while you were getting down here, in the whole three minutes I had, I did find a Glenda who married a Woodstock, and then they had two children, of which Mary was one, and Mary married a Blackwell."

"Blackwell."

"Yes, but I don't know if there are any relationships to Blackwells anywhere else."

Doreen muttered, "Blackwell, Blackwell. So, do you have any details on who the husband is?"

"Yes, he's here," she said. "That's what you were missing, isn't it?"

"Yes," Doreen replied. "I was just missing the name."

"So, he was a Blackwell, Cody Blackwell," she muttered, checking the files and then whistled. "And that marriage was, ... ooh, that was a long time ago, in 1976."

"That was a long time ago."

"And they had, ... let me keep looking here for children born of the marriage," she said, sifting through more files. "That'll be under the birth registries. Here it is," she said.

"There's the son, who is Eli," she noted, with a nod, "and a daughter born a few years later, and her name was Hope. Hope, *huh*? Nobody ever talks about Hope," she noted.

"Nobody ever talks about any of them from what I can determine," Doreen pointed out. "It seems as if the family was just unlucky, time and time again."

"Why is that?"

"Because the daughter also appeared to have been sick," Doreen added.

The librarian sighed. "Not a brain tumor issue too?"

"Yes, I think so," Doreen confirmed. "Eli was extremely tall and in a wheelchair for most of the time. After a car accident, I guess, he ended up with badly broken legs that didn't heal. He had some endocrine disorder discovered when his legs wouldn't heal, and that's when they found the brain tumor as well."

The librarian looked at her and muttered, "That's hardly fair, is it? He's suffered so much only to have that also be a part of his world."

"I know," Doreen agreed. "It's been a very strange case."

"They all are," she murmured, "but it never seems to matter."

"I couldn't find any obits on them."

"But now you have the last name."

"Right," Doreen agreed, pulling it up and sending a picture of it to Mack. Then she sent him a text, asking for anything on other Woodstock or Blackwell deaths.

He phoned her back and said, "Just because we have last names now doesn't mean I can get information that quickly. I'll check to see what we have under the DMV under those names, but I would need a little bit more information to confirm."

"Yeah, the information will be in the grave," she said.

First came silence on the other end. "You want to explain that?" he asked.

"Unfortunately I have a really ugly idea of what's going on," she replied. "And I hate to say it, but I have to run." She looked back at the librarian. "Thanks a lot." And, with that, Doreen bolted home again. There she grabbed all the animals. "I don't even know why I need you to come, except for the fact that it feels very much as if I need the talisman of having you around."

Thaddeus cried out, "Thaddeus is here. Thaddeus is here."

She laughed. "Exactly. Maybe that's all I need. Maybe you're my good luck charms," she murmured.

As she stepped outside, Mack was pulling up. She glared at him, and he glared right back.

"Wherever you're going, I'm coming too." He smiled as he saw the animals. "And I'm really glad you thought to bring them."

"I am to," she said in exasperation. "At this point in time, it feels as if they're my good luck charm."

"They probably are," he agreed, "so hop in."

She sighed. "You won't be very happy with me."

"What else is new?" he asked, with a laugh. "Your methods are unreasonable at best and crazy at the very least, but you do tend to get results. And when the captain heard me yelling at you to stop, he told me to go get you."

"Go get me, or go help me?"

"Same diff in his world." Mack laughed. "So here I am. Now, where are we going?"

"Back to the park."

"Of course we are," he grumbled. "Do you care to explain just what it is you think is going on?"

She sighed. "Since all the Woodstocks worked at Sky Manor, I think the old man found Eli after he fell out of his wheelchair. Or maybe the old guy was trying to move Eli and lost his hold on him, and Eli fell to his death. So I think the old guy feels guilty about Eli dying, but I don't think he actually killed him. However, … his wife probably knew where her husband buried Eli. In fact, she may have helped Welford carry the body to the park."

"And the sister?" Mack asked.

"I haven't worked that out yet. She could have just showed up at Sky Manor to visit Eli out of the blue, obviously after his death. Which led to her own. But …"

"But what?" Mack asked.

"I don't think the old man knew the sister was buried with her brother."

"So who killed the sister?"

Doreen groaned. "I'm working on that still."

The closer and closer they got to the park, she started to pivot and twist uneasily.

"What is wrong with you?" he cried out in exasperation.

She turned to him and asked, "Could you please go to another address instead?"

He glanced at her, catching the expression of horror on her face, and pulled out from where he was about to park and asked, "It's not very far from here, is it?"

"No, but I think it's probably already too far."

He shot her a look and turned on his siren. As soon as they got there, she bolted out of his truck, raced up to the front door, and knocked and knocked and knocked. She looked back at Mack. "Can we just go in?"

"If we have a reason to suspect that there's a problem."

"We do," she declared.

With that, he just shrugged, and, stepping back, he kicked in the door.

She raced in. "Meghan, Meghan, are you here?" she cried out, "Meghan?" She raced up to the bedroom, and there on the bed, a blanket over her and her hands folded on her chest, as if she had just laid down to rest, was Meghan. Doreen approached her cautiously. "Meghan, are you okay?"

Mack strode straight forward, pressed two fingers against her neck, looked over at Doreen, and shook his head.

She looked up at him and whispered, "I was too late. I just didn't get it in time."

"Easy, easy, easy," he muttered, as he looked around. "Are you telling me that this is not a natural death?"

"No, it's not a natural death," she said sadly. "It's definitely not."

He groaned. "Let me bring in the team. You are not going anywhere."

She nodded. "I'm not going anywhere. And, when I do go somewhere, I'm going with you." He looked at her, and she nodded. "I know the drill."

His lips twitched, and he nodded. "This is serious. We need answers."

"I know it is," she whispered. "And sometimes, sometimes that's all we ever have and what we can't get."

Chapter 27

DOREEN SAT IN Meghan's living room, as the crew came and went. Arnold stopped, looked at her, shook his head, and headed upstairs. She groaned, knowing that, as far as she was concerned, this was her fault.

"It's not your fault, you know," Elizabeth said from the doorway.

Doreen looked up and winced. "How did you know I was thinking that?"

"It's not hard since you're sitting here as if somebody just murdered your grandmother." Elizabeth grimaced. "And even when we have to do guesswork, like this," she added, "it still takes something to lead us to the right answers. Like this crime scene. ... Instinct is a lot of police work, ... yes, you seem to be using that in overdrive. I'm still not sure what is going on here," Elizabeth admitted, "but it could have been a suicide or it could be murder. I'll have to do a full workup first."

"Sleeping pills," Doreen muttered.

"Yes, that would be my guess, but we won't say that until we know for sure. I want to be certain before I pass any judgment on it."

"Of course." Doreen gave her a smile, but it was a sad smile.

Mack walked into the room, looked at her, and said, "I have to stay here."

She nodded. "I'll just sit outside in the garden for a little bit." She returned to the truck for the animals, knowing Mack was worried about her, then went outside to sit and commune with nature for a few minutes, maybe berate this life that had her getting here just a little too late.

She already knew the body was still warm. She already knew that she could have saved Meghan's life, but Doreen had missed that opportunity. Mack stepped out behind her. "You know that this isn't your fault."

She smiled at him. "I know that you guys will all tell me that, but I still feel that it's my fault."

"No. It's not. I don't know what's going on, and neither do you. We're doing as much guesswork as we possibly can to solve this, but that doesn't mean that we have answers yet," he explained, "so give yourself a break. Realize that this is part of the job. We make decisions. They're not always the easiest, and they're not always correct," he shared, "but we still have to get up and come back the next day and do it all over again."

She smiled at him. "And it just makes me appreciate you all that much more," she murmured. "Because it takes a special person to do this day in and day out, and, right now, I'm just sorry I ever heard about this case."

"That's what happens when all that excitement turns to work, and all the joy turns to sadness, and you realize just what's going on. We still don't know what's going on, and, while you might have an idea, you could be completely wrong."

She nodded. "I could be. … The sad part is, I'm pretty sure I now know what's going on, but I didn't put it together and get here in time to save her."

"Elizabeth also doesn't know if this was suicide or murder yet."

Doreen nodded. "I get that too. It would be nice if you found a letter or something in there. A letter would explain a lot."

"Would it?" he asked. "Or would it just completely confuse the issue?"

"I'm sure you'll look, and, if you see something, you can always let me know," she murmured.

"I'll see. It's you I'm worried about right now."

She looked at him, then shrugged. "I'm fine."

"No, … you're not. You're not fine at all. You're worried that you could have prevented this. Even worse, you're worried that you caused it, and I'm here to tell you, … *you didn't*. People do what they do, all on their own. They have free choice and free will, and that has nothing to do with you. So," he leaned over and gave her a gentle kiss and added, "just rest here for a bit, and then I'll take you home."

She watched him turn and walk back into the house. She got up, headed farther into the garden to the outdoor table and chairs with the animals, but then couldn't sit still so just wandered the yard. Surely she could have done something to make good on this. It all just seemed to be a colossal failure at the moment.

And, with that, she sat down on the grass, leaned against the fence, and just watched as the chaos from the house proceeded at a much more organized pace, but still one that contained all the fury and craziness of a murder. She heard sounds from the other side of the fence—whispers.

As she strained to hear more, Mugs started barking, and she quieted him down. It could be just noisy neighbors, or it could be anything. When a face popped over the top of the fence, she wondered. She crept closer, as Goliath hopped up on the fence and walked along the top. When she heard a *meow* and a hiss, she took a look over the fence and found Goliath.

A man stared at her and asked, "What's going on?"

"Don't worry about it," Doreen said. "It's got nothing to do with you."

He glared at her, then turned and walked away. But something was uncannily recognizable about him, and she called him back. "Hey, do you live around here?"

"Yeah, sure," he muttered.

"Why don't you come back and talk to me?"

He lifted a specific finger in the air, basically saying, *Absolutely no way.*

Then she smiled and nodded. As she sat back down again, she heard something else. A howl from the shrubbery. "Goliath, Goliath," she shrieked. She lifted Mugs and dropped him softly on the other side of the fence to help. Then she clambered over it herself. And the two of them raced to the bushes, where some cat fight was going on.

Then all of a sudden Goliath strode out, looking for the world as if he had just beaten something up.

She stared at him in shock. "Are you okay?" she cried out.

He just stared at her as if to say, *Don't be ridiculous.* But he had something in his mouth.

As Doreen got closer to him, Goliath dropped his find at her feet, a pill bottle, while some other cat took off through the bushes. She stared at the bottle, stared at the proximity to

Meghan's house, then called Mack on her phone.

"What's the matter?" he asked.

"Goliath found a pill bottle just over the fence."

"What are you talking about?" Mack looked out from the bedroom window.

Doreen waved at him, showing where she was, holding up a pill bottle. "Goliath found it."

"What do you mean, Goliath found it?" he asked in exasperation.

She shrugged and looked up at him. "I think Elizabeth should test this."

"I'm sure you do," he said. "I'll be there in a minute." He raced out, and it didn't take much for him to hop over the fence. He looked at the pill bottle and shook his head.

"Some guy was trying to ask me questions, but I didn't tell him anything."

"Good. Where is he now?"

"He took off."

"Of course he did. Any idea if he's the one who dropped the pill bottle?"

She looked at him and frowned. "I don't know."

"You need to show me where the pill bottle was." Mack quickly took some photos of the location of the pill bottle. As he glanced around, he added, "The cap is here too." Immediately he took photos of that, held it up, and then put the two together and nodded. "This could help, at least if we can prove that it had something to do with murder anyway. It does say it had sleeping pills in it."

"Yeah," Doreen agreed, "but look at the name on the prescription bottle." He stared at it and swore. She nodded. "It's the same couple."

"But why on earth? ... No, hang on a minute. There are

all kinds of reasons."

"Yeah, there sure could be. Maybe Meghan asked him if they had any pills, or maybe she told them, *Hey, I want to off myself. Do you have any sleeping pills I can add to my portfolio?*" she suggested in a caustic tone. "Or maybe they came over to have a confab about me *accusing them of something* and then dropped the pills into her tea or whatnot. I don't know," she muttered, glaring at him, "but obviously it's important."

"It is definitely important," he confirmed, with a nod. "Okay, I'll get this into evidence." He looked at her and added, "Then I'll take you home right after this."

"I'll just take Mugs for a bit of a walk around," she shared. "I think he's a little out of sorts that Goliath found something, and he didn't."

Mack just shook his head and added, "Stay close, please."

"Will do."

Not really wanting to climb back over the fence, she turned and headed in the direction that the young man had gone. Of course, he wasn't that young. He had to be fortysomething. Mugs was tugging her faster and faster, and she raced behind him, knowing that he was on the scent of something. As she followed Mugs out to the street again, she realized they were on a cul-de-sac, with no way out.

She stopped, looked around, and nodded. "Okay. So you brought me here," she murmured. "Did you realize that's what you were doing?"

Just then the same man appeared in front of her, frowning. "What are you doing here still?"

"I found your pill bottle in the bushes back there."

He paled and glared at her. "I don't know what you're

talking about."

"Yeah? That was one of the parts that confused me, and I didn't understand how anybody in their condition could do all this, or why they even would."

"I don't know what you're talking about," the stranger snapped, "and you need to just shut up and leave me alone."

"I'm not really very good at that," she noted, staring at him. "I mean, if you knew me better, you would understand that I am a challenge for everybody in my circle of friends."

"You're not in *my* circle of friends," he declared, "and I can't say I would ever want you in my circle of friends. So I really don't care what you have to say."

She smiled at him and added, "I think you will care. So, are you a Woodstock or are you a Blackwell?"

He frowned at her and then glanced around. "That's not funny."

"I don't see anything funny about any of this," she said. "I don't know what your role is in any of this, other than the muscle man, but none of it is good news."

"I don't even know what you're talking about," he muttered. "You need to get out of my face."

"Maybe," she conceded, "maybe I do. You can bet Mack would tell me that I need to."

"Mack who?" he asked. "Lady, are you okay? Do you need to be hospitalized or something?"

She smiled. "Lots of people would say so."

Then she heard something she was already half expecting.

Chapter 28

THE OLD MAN stepped out from the bushes, glaring at her. "What are you doing here?" Welford roared. Then he charged toward her, his fist curled, as if ready to strike her.

She stood her ground and stared at him. "Is that what you do?"

"What do you mean?" he asked, frozen at the question.

"I mean, do you scare people so they take off and run?"

"Don't you mock me," he cried out. "In my day … I was important."

"Maybe," she muttered. "Maybe not anymore."

The stranger pointed a finger at Doreen. "Hey, hey, hey, stop. That's enough."

Doreen snorted. "Yeah, … please stop interrupting. Welford was just about to confess."

"As if," the stranger barked, staring at her.

"I don't have anything to confess," Welford declared.

"See?" the stranger barked.

Doreen shook her head. "*Right.* You mean Gramps is doing it all by himself?"

At that, the stranger's face flushed, turned all kinds of

ugly, and he glared at her. "I don't know who you are, what you are, or what you think you're doing here," he began in a very low tone, "but whatever accusations you think you'll get away with, you won't."

It took Doreen a moment to decode all that and then nodded. "Is that what you think?"

"She's dangerous. Get away from her," the old man cried out, "and she's not all there."

Doreen smiled at him. "That's how you've got everybody bamboozled, isn't it, Welford?"

He frowned at her. "You don't know what you're talking about."

"Maybe not, but I'm really close to figuring it out. You know what I think? I think you made an arrangement with Eli's father to look after Eli—and potentially his sister—for money."

He blinked at her, and a stillness came over him. "You don't know anything. And, even if I did, what's that got to do with anything?"

"You haven't heard all I want to say. I don't know how you managed it, but Canada was no longer paying for Eli's care at Sky Manor. How did you get the government to send that money to you? I'm really curious to find out. I'm sure the government would like to know more about that too. So, you worked your magic, and the father somehow directed the government money into your bank account for the care of Eli. And then you decided that maybe you shouldn't have to do all that work looking after Eli."

At that, the younger man interrupted, "Whoa, whoa, whoa. I don't like where you're going with this," he snapped at her. "Don't even think like that."

"Oh, it's far too late for that. This is how my mind

works. I couldn't figure out what it would take to have somebody treat Eli so badly. I mean, what kind of person would do something like that? All Eli wanted was a chance at a life. That's all he needed, just a normal life. But here you guys are, putting Eli in an early grave, and not even a grave that anybody would know about. No, no, no, that would be too easy. Instead, you were keeping all that government money, piling it away, and nobody would know the difference. You didn't want anybody to find out that the money for Eli's care was not used for Eli, as he was dead almost thirty years ago, right? So all that money you were spending for your own care. I mean, it was one thing to take it while you could, but why do the work too? It was so much easier to just kill Eli."

"I didn't kill him," Welford cried out. "I didn't kill Eli."

Doreen stared at him. "I hope not," she murmured. "I really do, because you'll pay the price if you did."

"I didn't kill him," he repeated. "It wasn't my fault. He fell. He fell out of his wheelchair and into the bathtub. It wasn't my fault, I swear."

"So, you just shoved him in the ground like some garbage, like a dead plant? You shove it in the ground, and either it lives or dies?"

"You don't understand anything. And I don't know how Hope got there."

"Oh, but I do. You couldn't afford to let anybody know that Eli was gone. You even buried his old X-ray in the grave with him. Erased all signs of him in life. *But* you couldn't afford to let anybody know what was happening—not the government and not the siblings' father, if he's still alive. You needed that money, didn't you?"

The old man's face worked several times, and his shoulders seemed to finally give up the ghost of protest. And he visibly sagged in place. "You don't know what it's like," he muttered.

"I hear that time and time again from various people." She pulled out her phone and sent a text to Mack.

Immediately the young man grabbed her phone and tossed it. "You don't need that," he grumbled. "No way you're getting out of this."

"Oh, *right*," she exclaimed, with a smile. "You must be on the same gravy train. You do know, at some point in time, people get too old to get government checks. And that time is coming, but you needed to get something else in place first."

"Lady, all you speak is gibberish to me."

"Not to him," Doreen stated, as she pointed to the old man. "Welford understands because the old man here is getting too old to keep up the pretense. He didn't have much of a pretense anyway," she declared. Turning to the stranger, she added, "And neither do you. I mean, there's no reason you can't work, is there?"

He stared at her. "You're a little too nosy for your own good." He stared down at the animals. "And what is with that dog?"

He was once again sniffing around the old man's pant legs. Welford kicked at Mugs, but Mugs was wise enough to stay out of kicking distance. "I told you to keep him away from me," he roared.

"Your wife told me that you've supposedly got a catheter bag in there, but I don't think so. I'm not sure what Mugs is smelling except for a liar, cheater, murderer, and fraudster. I mean, he does have a good nose for that sort of thing."

Welford glared at her. "You can't prove nothing."

"Oh, we couldn't for sure before, but now we can. We absolutely can. I hate to say it, but the gig is up, guys. Did you really have to kill Meghan though?"

They stopped and stared.

She nodded. "I found the prescription pill bottle that your nephew"—and watched the acknowledgement slid into the old man's gaze—"threw away. I didn't even hear him in Meghan's house. Presumably I interrupted him when I came barging in, yelling her name."

The young man looked uneasily over at the old man.

"He threw the pill bottle in the bushes behind here." Doreen pointed.

The old man shrugged. "He didn't have nothing to do with anything."

"The thing is, that pill bottle he threw has your name on it."

He stared at her and shook his head. "It doesn't matter. I gave Meghan the pills."

"No, but what you did do was give her a bit of money to keep her quiet."

His bottom lip curled. "You don't know what you're talking about."

"Yes, I do." Doreen continued. "Meghan was blackmailing you, making sure she got a piece of the action, and you guys were getting poorer and poorer. You were getting more broke as the cost of living went up. That government money was your income. That and your little bit from the Canada Pension Plan. I mean, you've been sitting here cheating the government for so many years, and you couldn't even give Eli a decent burial. He was a good man, and he just needed a little bit of time on this earth to make it an even better place."

The old man cried out, "You don't know anything."

"No, I don't. In many ways, I certainly don't," she agreed. "Yet in some ways I already know way too much."

"You're right about that," the nephew declared, staring at her. "I don't know who you are, or who you think you are, but you can't just come over here and start making up stuff."

"Oh, but I know what you two did, so I can talk all I want," she stated, with a nod in his direction. "And obviously you were privy to the whole thing. I mean, you were getting your cut of the con too, right? … Do you even work, or do you just sit around and steal from people? Help your elderly relatives bury people in the park?"

He glared at her and took several steps forward. Mugs growled at him and then started barking like crazy. "Shut him up, or I'll kick him and hurt him bad," the nephew roared.

"You can try," Doreen replied, "but I've got to tell you that they've really gotten a bad reputation around here."

"What? Your *pets* are dangerous?" the nephew asked, with a snort. "You've got a cat on a freaking leash. And it's not even on the leash right now. You just let it run loose? That's disgusting."

"Maybe." She looked over at the old man. "What about your wife? Where is she now?"

"She's in the house," he said, staring at her, "and it's none of your business."

"Of course not. You really think I didn't tell the cops where I was going?" His jaw worked, and she nodded. "The gig is up, and I told you that. And that big *caregiver* paycheck you've been getting all this time? Yeah, you won't be getting that anymore."

"It doesn't matter. I'm dying anyway," he grumbled.

"Oh, not a moment too soon, is that it? I mean, you took all the money for the care supposedly going to Eli, for him to have a life, and then you bury him out in the park." Welford glared at her. "And you've been collecting that money for a very long time."

His bottom jaw firmed up, and he added, "I don't have to listen to you."

"Maybe not, but what about Eli's sister?" she asked.

"What about his sister? What about her?" he asked, staring at her.

"She was buried in the same grave."

He stared at her, shook his head, and muttered, "That's not possible."

"Oh, … but it is. It absolutely is," she stated. "I figured you must have been getting the checks for her care too."

"No, no, I wasn't," he said, confused, "not at all."

Just then the door opened, and his wife came out, glaring at Doreen. "You couldn't leave well enough alone, could you?"

"Nope." Doreen gave her a wry smile. "It's an occupational hazard."

"You're just a nosy busybody."

Doreen nodded. "That too, and I get it. I mean, I really get it. You're probably pissed off that I'm here."

"Yeah, you're not kidding," Mrs. Woodstock snapped. "You don't belong here, and you don't need to be here."

"If I wasn't here, I would be down at the police station, telling them everything. In the meantime, the cops are all over at your *friend's* house."

"She's not our friend," Mrs. Woodstock snapped.

"That's because she was blackmailing you. … After all,

Meghan didn't have an income either."

Mrs. Woodstock eyed Doreen resentfully.

Doreen nodded. "I get it. I mean, it was hard enough to live on that money, and then, with all the inflation and the blackmail payment and everything else, it was getting worse, wasn't it? It's bad enough that Eli was in that grave the whole time and that you guys buried him there," she muttered.

The older woman stared at her, totally clear-eyed.

"But then you killed Eli's sister," Doreen added, noting no remorse at all coming from Mrs. Woodstock. "As far as I know, the sister, although she may have had a brain tumor, that doesn't mean that she died from it. I'm still awaiting the autopsy report."

Mrs. Woodstock glanced at her husband, then back at Doreen. "You don't know what you're talking about."

"Yeah, see? That's the problem," she pointed out. "I might not know everything, but I know an awful lot."

"You know too much," the young man snapped.

She looked at him and nodded. "For you probably, yes, because your aunt and uncle won't necessarily live very much longer. Now you on the other hand? You will spend a fair bit of time in jail."

"I won't go to jail," he declared, glaring at her.

"It's called theft, fraud, and murder," Doreen noted. "So, I'm not sure what planet you're living on, but all of those things are illegal."

He took two steps toward her, and she backed up, almost falling in her rush to avoid him, and he laughed. "Look at you. You're just a little scared busybody."

"I'm hardly scared of you, though you're way bigger than I am and could definitely cause me some harm. I'm sure Eli's sister really didn't appreciate being threatened by you either."

Welford roared, "We didn't touch the sister."

Doreen studied him, and, with a sadness that came from the heart, she stated, "You might not have, but these two did. They killed Hope."

He blinked at her, then turned to his wife and to the young man at her side.

Doreen pointed. "Just look at them. You can see the truth in their eyes." Doreen looked at the wife and said, "This is your nephew, I presume."

She nodded.

"And the sister came looking for her brother, didn't she? But you couldn't have that, could you? You couldn't have Hope telling everybody that Eli wasn't here. You couldn't have her saying things about Eli, causing someone to come and investigate, could you?"

"But what were we supposed to do?" Mrs. Woodstock cried out. "There wasn't any choice."

Welford turned to stare at his wife. "You didn't tell me."

"No, because you wouldn't be happy about it."

"Of course I wouldn't be happy about it," he bellowed. "What we did wasn't against the person, it was just the government."

Doreen laughed at that. "Of course. Who cares about defrauding the government? I mean, they steal from you guys all the time with taxes, right?"

"Yes," he agreed, "exactly. And we never hurt anybody. But …" He turned to face his wife and his nephew and saw the truth in their eyes. "Good God."

"Exactly," Doreen murmured. "*Good God*, that poor woman died because she came to see her brother, for whatever reason, needing to reconnect. She wanted to see her brother, and that's a lovely sentiment," Doreen noted. "But you couldn't even let her do that, could you?"

Mrs. Woodstock shook her head. "We couldn't. We would have ended up in jail for the rest of our lives if she sounded the alarm."

"News flash, lady, you'll still end up behind bars."

"Maybe," she said resentfully. "But, at this age, it won't be for very long. Even Welford here has very few days left."

"You know what'll happen in those days?" Doreen asked. "You and the rest of your family here are about to find out." She turned and looked at the young man, who even now stared at Mugs, then looked around, as if seeking an escape route. She smiled at him and said, "You can run, but you can't hide."

He snorted. "You don't know me, lady."

"No, I don't know you, but I do know my animals."

He frowned at her. "You think *these* will stop me?" He laughed. "No way."

She smiled. "I get that your aunt and uncle are too old to run, but they aren't too old to tattle on you. I get that you think that they won't because they're family, but just look at Welford here. He's not very happy about what you and his wife did to Eli's sister."

"No," Welford confirmed, staring at his wife in shock. "That is just too much," he said, shaking his head. "How could you do that?"

She stared at him. "It's not as if we had enough money to live on," she explained, shaking her head. "What was I supposed to do?"

There were tears in Welford's eyes, and his wife finally realized that she had misjudged him. He really did separate out the good and the bad in his life, and, in his twisted way of thinking, the government or the rich were fair game to defraud.

It wasn't the first time Doreen had heard that sentiment.

Welford had no idea what his wife and his nephew were capable of. It was literally right there in his expression.

"I'm sorry for you because your wife and your nephew are murderers," Doreen proclaimed. "And, for that, they will pay the price, but everybody will know what you guys have done, and you will be tarred by the same brush."

Welford slowly shook his head. "She was a nice girl," he muttered, turning to look at Doreen. And this time the tears dripped from the corner of his eyes.

"Yes, *she was a nice girl*," the wife stated, "but I had no choice."

"There's always a choice," Doreen noted.

"Oh, for crying out loud," the nephew yelled.

She looked at him and noted, "I don't even know what your name is."

"His name is Welford too," Welford shared. "He was named after me."

"*Right*," she muttered, "a chip off the old block. And now that chip will spend a long time in jail."

At that, Welford Junior bolted. She looked at Mugs and said, "Go."

With Mugs barking away, racing behind him, Junior headed down the block. Mugs was catching up, getting closer and closer. Just as Mugs was about to get him, Goliath raced ahead and took a flying leap, landing on the back of Junior's shirt, sending him screaming to the ground in agony, Goliath's claws digging into his back all the way.

"Oh my God," Mrs. Woodstock cried out. "Stop, stop."

"There's no stopping," Doreen announced, "but don't worry. All kinds of people will be stopping in any minute now."

Sure enough, Mack tore into view on foot, stopping when he saw Goliath sharpening his claws on the man's back and Mugs's teeth wrapped around the man's ankle. Mack looked over at Doreen, his hands on his hips, and asked, "Where the heck is Thaddeus?"

Thaddeus poked his head out from Doreen's hair and cried out, "Thaddeus is here. Thaddeus is here."

Mack looked at him and sighed. "How come you're not having part of the fun?"

Thaddeus flew down to strut all over Junior's shoulders and arms. "Thaddeus is here. Thaddeus is here."

"Too little, too late, Thaddeus," Doreen cried out.

He glared at her and said, "Thaddeus is king. Thaddeus is king."

"Oh my," she muttered. "Who the heck taught him that?" Then she turned and glared at Mack.

"Don't look at me," he said, raising both hands in mock surrender. "That would be Nan. They were playing some game, and she told him that he was the king to her queen or something like that."

Doreen laughed and laughed. "Thaddeus, in this case, maybe you are the king."

He cackled. "King of the castle. King of the castle."

Mrs. Woodstock declared, "He's demented."

"He might be," Doreen conceded, "but, even if he's demented, he's my kind of demented." She glared at the older woman. "He doesn't cheat. He doesn't steal, and he surely doesn't hurt anybody."

"He's hurting my nephew," she snapped.

"In that case, I would reckon it's well deserved." She looked over at Mack and said, "You won't believe it."

He glared at her. "I'm sure I won't. Yet, after seeing

what's going on here"—he pointed to Mugs, Goliath, and Welford the younger—"I guess I'm about to hear it anyway."

She quickly laid it out, and he stared at the trio in shock. "Good God." Then he looked back in the direction of the house where he had just come from. "What about her? What's her connection?"

"Meghan's been blackmailing them all this time," Doreen shared, "but her conscience kicked in, and she realized that, since she was about ready to die herself, she wanted to clear her conscience. She had cancer, was seeing an oncologist."

Mack stared at Doreen, then looked at the others.

The old man nodded. "I didn't have the heart to argue with Meghan. I'm just tired," he admitted.

"Yeah, well, how much heart did you have when it came to killing Meghan?" Mack asked.

He shook his head. "That wasn't me." He waved at his wife. "That was these two."

Doreen looked at Welford and asked, "Are you sure about that?"

He nodded. "I draw the line at killing people," he muttered. "I might be old and cranky, but I still wouldn't ever hurt anybody like that." He turned and glared at his wife. "But her, on the other hand? She's got a mean streak a mile wide."

She snorted. "I absolutely do, and it's one that you've loved all these years."

"I know," he admitted, sadness in his gaze, "but, at some point, you've just got to stop."

Mack asked, "Has she killed anybody else?"

He frowned at his wife and replied, "I didn't know about her killing Hope. That was Eli's sister, so you'll have to ask her."

Mrs. Woodstock shook her head. "Only self-preservation put me into that position in the first place."

Doreen wasn't sure if she believed them or not. She turned to Mack and noted, "I think we're finally getting somewhere."

"Getting somewhere, or is it done?"

"This part's done," she said, "but I haven't found the senator's daughter." She paused, then turned to Mrs. Woodstock. "Unless you killed her too."

"No," she cried out, "I don't know anything about her."

"What about your nephew?"

"No, he's not into anything that gets his hands dirty."

At that, the old man snorted. "He's also not into anything that resembles work."

"*Right*," Doreen muttered, "so I'm guessing he really didn't appreciate burying Eli's sister in the same grave."

"I can't believe you did that," Mr. Woodstock whispered, turning to his wife.

She shrugged.

He shook his head, then looked back at Doreen. "I'm sorry. Hope was a lovely girl."

"Yeah, she was. She also fought hard with her own health issues. Too bad she didn't realize that the real danger in her world was coming from the people who were supposedly looking after her beloved brother."

Chapter 29

MACK LIFTED HIS teacup and clinked it with hers. "That one ended up more than a little crazy."

"It did," Doreen agreed, "but, at the end of the day, it's still all about human greed."

"And, in this case, fear as well."

"It's all ultimately about greed," she repeated. "I mean, I get it. They were facing an uncertain old age, but to cheat and kill like that? I don't understand."

"And murdering Eli's sister."

"That was the wife. I'm wondering how any of that will play out in court," she said. "Though that's really not an interest for me."

He laughed. "Maybe not, but believe me that the captain's crowing about it. He did however …"

"I know. I know." She groaned. "He asked me about it too."

"It *is* a cold case, and it's definitely one we need help on," he admitted. "I sure wish I knew how your brain worked."

"I didn't make that Meghan connection with Eli's case. I really only got that part when I saw the pill bottle."

"Really?" he asked. "Not until then?"

"Nope, not until then. I was tossing all kinds of options back and forth, but that was the clincher."

"How was that a clincher?"

"Because there had to be a reason to kill Meghan, and the only reason I could see was if she knew something, and, if she knew something, what could that possibly be, and what was the reason behind it. Then it just fell into place from there. Money seemed to be an issue, even back to the very first time I met the older couple. That kept festering in my mind. We didn't even confirm Eli's full name properly until today. So we had no way to know yet if he was still on the books for government assistance, which would have led to checks being paid somewhere else, somewhere other than Sky Manor."

She shrugged. "I don't know if the government still pays for those services, but they supposedly shut down for a while, kicking people out of these homes. I don't have all the details on that. Still, if we had gone down this pathway a little further, we may have seen that Welford Woodstock was getting checks deposited into his account for Eli's care, either via the government fund or via Eli's own father. Either way, that revelation would have led to more evidence when you followed that trail."

"Right." Mack nodded. "We would have found out quite simply that he was getting a check for the care of a disabled person who was dead long ago," he noted.

"Once the old couple knew the body would likely be identified as that of Eli, the Woodstocks began to panic over money, and things began to erode, causing them all to act a bit suspiciously, which is what drew me to them in the first place."

"You sure have good instincts and the ability to get people to talk, even when they don't want to."

"I was really floundering this time, trying to make it all fit. All the while, nothing pulled together to make sense," she shared.

"What do you mean, *this time*?" Mack laughed. "It's not even that you floundered. It's just, when you do guess, you tend to be very on the mark."

"I'll say *thank you* for that," she conceded, with a laugh, "but you and I both know that, lots of times, I don't find out anything for sure until the very last minute, and then it's just plain scary."

"I won't argue with that because, every time I turn around, I see Mugs and Goliath attacking people. Then I know the bad guys have gone after you, and, if they've gone after you, it's usually for a darn-good reason."

She glared at him, but he nodded. "You are threatening to incarcerate them for the rest of their life, and that scares people, so they'll do anything they can to avoid it. And that generally means hurting you."

"I know," she said, "and I'm sorry for scaring you."

"When I heard Mugs barking, I just ran."

"And look at that," she said, beaming at him. "Just look at how well trained you are."

"How well trained I am?" he repeated, looking at her in horror.

"Mugs barked, and you came running," she pointed out, with a chuckle. "I mean, it's just perfect."

"No, it's not perfect at all. Mugs is the one that's supposed to be trained. You're supposed to give him a command, and then he comes running."

She looked back at Mugs, a twinkle in her eyes. "I think he missed that part."

"Ya think?" Mack groaned. "You guys will be the death of me, I swear."

"Nope, we won't," she declared, with a big grin, "but we will keep your life interesting."

He snatched her up into his arms and held her close. "That you will," he confirmed, "but please look after yourself."

"I promise."

He rolled his eyes. "Don't make promises you won't keep."

"I'll try to promise."

He stared at her and shook his head. "That's not help-ing."

She burst out laughing. "I'll go back to work on the other missing person's case, the senator's daughter. But just think, we've now solved several of them."

"We have, indeed."

Just then her phone buzzed with a text message, and she glanced down at it. "Oh, that's the mother of the young woman who was buried under the wrong name. She wants to take me out for coffee."

When Mack frowned, Doreen shrugged. "She'd already heard about me from Elizabeth. So, when I reached out to give her my condolences, she wanted to connect."

"That's nice." Mack nodded, then frowned, "Unless she's looking for you to solve another murder."

"I don't think so." Doreen giggled. "She just wants to take me out as a *thank you*."

"That's good," Mack said, "and I don't have a problem with that."

"I'm glad to hear it," she declared in an exaggerated tone.

He rolled his eyes. "You do know that, if I had my way, I would keep you under lock and key."

"Ah, but, if the captain had his way," she added, a big grin on her face, "he would have a spare key made so he could keep me working."

At that, Mack burst out laughing. "You're probably correct there."

She smiled, then kissed him. "Thank you for always being there."

He stared at her and sighed. "What if I'm not always there? Do you know how many nightmares you'll give me?"

She blinked. "I hadn't considered that."

"I know. You never do. But, for me, it's a constant worry."

"I am working on being safer. The animals are working on being more proactive, and you're working on your training."

"My training," he repeated, turning to glare at her.

She shrugged and, with a double-wattage grin, added, "What can I say? You're doing great with it."

Epilogue

SEVERAL NIGHTS LATER, as Mack and Doreen were cuddling up together after dinner, his phone rang. "Hello, Captain. … Yeah, I'm here with Doreen now. … I know. I know. We've just been discussing it. It's pretty sad."

The captain spoke for several minutes, the smile falling off Mack's face.

"Right, another murder," he muttered, turning all business. "No, I'm coming. … Yeah, I'll head down to the office. What do we know?"

Doreen leaned in to hear, but he hopped to his feet and glared at her.

"Right, sorry," she whispered.

"Okay. … Oh, okay." He frowned. "No, I'll be there in just a few minutes." He reached out a hand and helped Doreen to her feet, as he ended the call. "I've got to go," he said.

"A new case?" she asked, watching him sideways. "Any details?"

"No," he declared, glaring at her. "No details, specifically none for you."

"Why not?" she wailed.

"Because it's not a cold case. And, besides, you've got to work on yours. The senator's daughter, remember?"

"Sure, and I will, but I can't believe you've already got another one."

"I do, but it doesn't sound like a whole lot of fun though."

"Why is that?"

"A restaurant kitchen is the crime scene," he replied. "A man and a woman were working on a catering job. Apparently the man's been stabbed."

"Oh, wow," Doreen muttered, as she stared at him. "What was the weapon?"

"Don't know for sure. … They think it was a knife from the kitchen."

"Ah."

Mack groaned.

"What?" she asked.

"You won't believe it."

"But I do believe it."

He winced. "I think the captain mentioned they found the knife in a … watermelon."

"Watermelon?" she repeated, looking at him in shock. "Oh, cutting up the watermelon itself?"

"Maybe. I think so," he said, "but, until I get there, I won't know the details."

"Just remember to keep me posted," Doreen stated, with a bright smile.

"No way," he replied. "It's got nothing to do with you. It's a current case. *My* current case."

"It could involve me though."

"No, it can't. It's an active case."

"It's an active case, *but* …" She beamed.

"What?" he asked, frowning at her.

"It's a *Weapon in the Watermelon*."

He closed his eyes, swore under his breath, and muttered, "Okay, I'll give you that one, but it's still my case, and you stay out of it."

Then he leaned over, kissed her hard, and headed for his truck.

This concludes Book 3 of Lovely Lethal Gardens Rewind: X-Ray in the Xanth.

Read about Weapon in the Watermelon: Lovely Lethal Gardens Rewind, Book 4

Lovely Lethal Gardens Rewind: Weapon in the Watermelon (Book 4)

When a young couple is attacked while prepping for a catering job, it seems like the family is dealing with a long running curse. One that ends in murder… Doreen can't stop meddling and when she finds out that that the young woman's mother is an unsolved murder case she has her way into the investigation.

But like all her cases, nothing is quite so simple. While Mack is dealing with the death of the dead chef, Doreen is working behind the scenes to sort out all different family factions while also trying to sort out a gift for Nan's birthday yet somehow she managed to mix the two together.

Now if only things would go smoothly from here on in—but of course not. With the animals involved the chaos is even wilder.

Find Weapon in the Watermelon here!
To find out more visit Dale Mayer's website.
https://geni.us/DMSWeapon

Author's Note

Thank you for reading X-Ray in the Xanth: Lovely Lethal Gardens Rewind, Book 3! If you enjoyed the book, please take a moment and leave a short review.

Dear reader,

I love to hear from readers, and you can contact me at my website: www.dalemayer.com or at my Facebook author page. To be informed of new releases and special offers, sign up for my newsletter or follow me on BookBub. And if you are interested in joining Dale Mayer's Reader Group, here is the Facebook sign up page.
http://geni.us/DaleMayerFBGroup

Cheers,
Dale Mayer

About the Author

Dale Mayer is a *USA Today* best-selling author, best known for her SEALs military romances, her Psychic Visions series, and her Lovely Lethal Garden cozy series. Her contemporary romances are raw and full of passion and emotion (Broken But … Mending, Hathaway House series). Her thrillers will keep you guessing (Kate Morgan, By Death series), and her romantic comedies will keep you giggling (*It's a Dog's Life*, a stand-alone novella; and the Broken Protocols series, starring Charming Marvin, the cat).

Dale honors the stories that come to her—and some of them are crazy, break all the rules and cross multiple genres!

To go with her fiction, she also writes nonfiction in many different fields, with books available on résumé writing, companion gardening, and the US mortgage system. All her books are available in print and ebook format.

Connect with Dale Mayer Online

Dale's Website – www.dalemayer.com
Twitter – @DaleMayer
Facebook Page – geni.us/DaleMayerFBFanPage
Facebook Group – geni.us/DaleMayerFBGroup
BookBub – geni.us/DaleMayerBookbub
Instagram – geni.us/DaleMayerInstagram
Goodreads – geni.us/DaleMayerGoodreads
Newsletter – geni.us/DaleNews